RICH
OR DEAD

RICH
OR DEAD

by Michael Cormany

An Irma Heldman /Birch Lane Press Book
Published by Carol Publishing Group

CORMANY, M.

Copyright © 1990 by Michael Cormany

A Birch Lane Press Book
Published by Carol Publishing Group

Editorial Offices
600 Madison Avenue
New York, NY 10022

Sales & Distribution Offices
120 Enterprise Ave.
Secaucus, NJ 07094

In Canada: Musson Book Company
A division of General Publishing Co. Limited
Don Mills, Ontario

Manufactured in the United States of America

Library of Congress Cataloging-in-Publication Data

Cormany, Michael.
      Rich or dead / by Michael Cormany.
          p,   cm.
      "An Irma Heldman / Birch Lane Press book."
      ISBN 1-55972-024-7
      I. Title..
    PS3553.06525R5   1990
    813'.54--dc20   89-71167
                              CIP

RICH
OR DEAD

ONE

A slob-bellied man with a blond crew cut hated Chicago so bad he was proud of it. Needed to brag about it to everybody in the bar. Like a high school Hamlet, he waved his arms and declaimed in a squeaky voice, "This Cheecawgoh of yours is the asshole of the U.S. of A. were anybody to ask me. I been here eight weeks, I ain't worked one single day, ain't found one card game on the square, ain't got my rocks off, nothin'." He lifted his drink, looked at it. "For Godsakes, I can't even find a decent Scotch and soda in this shithole."

I paused behind the slob's back, grateful he wasn't the man I was searching for. According to Elvia Reyes, the man I wanted was Stacey Ford. Slim build, all over freckles on pasty skin, sandy hair slipping into blue eyes, sparse mustache. A man who fit that description was staring into a glass of beer at the far end of the bar, right where Elvia said he'd be.

She also claimed this guy was as mean as a cornered wolverine. So when I got behind him I grabbed both bony shoulders and yanked him backwards off the stool. Took him straight down to the floor on his back. His arms bounced straight out at his sides like he was preparing to make angels in snow. I scampered around to his side, sank my left knee into his belly, pinned his left bicep with my right knee, jammed my left index and middle fingers into his throat just below his voice box, and raised my right fist above my head.

He looked up at me, eyes wide with shock. I said, "My name is Dan Kruger. I'm pleased to meet you, Ford. I apologize for this. Please don't think I lack the social graces. Normally I introduce myself to a stranger with a firm handshake and a warm hello like the true gentleman I am. But in a fair fight I ain't worth a damn and I understand you are one ornery customer. Tell me where Elvia Reyes' brother is."

He tried to suck in some air, started to gag. I lifted my fingers for a second. He croaked, "Who?" His Adam's apple quivered

1

against my fingernails and the pressure on his voice box made him sound like a munchkin.

"Ricardo Reyes. You know him."

"So what?"

"Where is he?"

"I dunno. How the hell should I know?"

"Because he's your friend."

"You tell me where every friend you got is right this minute."

"Wouldn't be hard. Where does Reyes stay?"

"I ain't seen him over a week."

I shifted my hundred and forty pounds and made like I planned to push my knee through Ford's stomach and spine right into the floor. I gripped his voice box with my fingertips, gave it a firm squeeze. He flopped his arms and I released the pressure. He rasped, "Okay, okay, stop. He's at the Elizabeth."

As I hurried out I heard the slob at the bar yelling, "You see? You see what kind of shit I'm talking about?"

The Elizabeth Hotel is a flophouse west of the Loop. One of the few left now that the commodity traders and lawyers and money managers are making over Chicago and sticking luxury high rise apartments all over the place, including where the skid rows used to be. The lobby is slightly bigger than a bread box and smells like a Comiskey Park men's room after a double-header. I banged on the mesh cage that runs the length of the five foot sign in desk. A shrunken old man wearing a dirty Cubs cap and a dirtier blue work shirt shuffled out from a back room that had a nailed-up blanket for a door. With no expression on his face, he studied the photograph I slid at him, then said, "I would like to see some ID or a sawbuck, if you don't mind. Preferably the latter."

I held my PI photostat against the wire in front of the man's eyes. Said, "I know the man's name is Ricardo Reyes. I know for a fact he's here so don't play coy and stall for money. I got none."

He leaned forward to read. As he did his lip curled. He breathed through his mouth and a bubble of spit at the corner of his lips inflated and deflated with each breath. After some seconds he said, "This spic ain't wanted for no felony, is he?"

"Relax, Pops, no reward. There'd be real law here if he was wanted. His sister's looking for him, that's all. She's an illegal so she can't go to the cops."

"Lousy wetbacks," he muttered. "Reyes is 214." He flicked the photo through the hole in the bottom of the cage and turned for the back room.

Room 214 was halfway down the second floor corridor on the left. I knocked three times, waited. No response. I twisted the knob, pushed the door with my foot. It creaked open.

Ricardo Reyes lay on his back on the floor at the foot of the bed. He was dead and not by natural causes. Natural causes don't leave knife-sliced necks that squirt pools of blood big as Lake Michigan on the floor.

There were two things Elvia Reyes had wanted: her brother and the brown paper shopping bag he had with him.

Being careful not to step in the blood, which was mostly on his right side because that's the side his head lolled to, I did a rapid frisk of Reyes and then tossed the room. I didn't think the bag would be there, but I needed to make sure. I slid open dresser drawers and skimmed my hand under the thin mattress, then under the seat cushion of a grimy green chair, then peered into what passed for a closet. While I searched I cursed myself for showing the deskman my license instead of slipping him the ten spot. Now I'd have to report a murder.

I found nothing. Not even a cheap bottle of Tequila or a Gideon's Bible.

As I trudged down the stairs to phone the police, I asked myself what in hell could have been in that paper bag that someone would carve up an illegal alien to get it?

TWO

But Elvia Reyes wouldn't be telling me what it was because she was gone.

After a short discussion with myself, I had decided to relate the truth—minus the paper bag part—to the cops who eventually showed at the Elizabeth. One knifed-up illegal Mex didn't unduly concern any of them, but a detective decided a uniform man should check my story so their respective asses would be covered in case it turned out I was involved in something important. The uniform man's name was Dezler. He was immensely obese, wore a Dick Nixon five o'clock shadow over three chins. He started grumbling soon as I got in his squad car, making clear this was a job he could live without and nicely.

The address Elvia had given me was a tar paper shingle frame on 17th Street in Pilsen, Chicago's main Hispanic neighborhood. Adjacent to the house was a rubbish filled vacant lot. On the other side of the lot was an abandoned grocery store. On the side of the store was a handpainted mural in red and orange and yellow and blue showing Jesus Christ blessing many diverse citizens of Estados Unidos Mexicanos, Pancho Villa in particular. He was drawn almost as big as Jesus. I liked it. I like most of the murals that are all over Pilsen. Bold colors, unique perspectives—they're always interesting. But Dezler said, "Why the fuck do beaners think they got to slap a huge, ugly-as-shit painting on the side of every building they see?" I did not explain to him the influence Diego Rivera had on the Mexican artistic psyche because Dezler obviously would not care.

A short, chunky woman, Mrs. Salazar, owned the house. She let us in because of Dezler's uniform, allowed us to look around. She didn't have to of course, but she didn't know that. She shook her head when I said I wanted to talk to Elvia Reyes. She said, "No one that name here." So I repeated my question louder and slower like Anglo's do when speaking to someone whose English is poor. Quicker than Berlitz, slow shouting is.

I showed her the photo of Ricardo. Said, still loudly, "She looks like him sort of, but younger. She's maybe twenty-two, very skinny, got long thin lips go halfway round her face, no hips, small chest." I illustrated each characteristic with hand gestures. "She dyed her hair blonde and it looks two tone now because the black roots are out a couple inches and the blonde didn't take all over so there's lotsa black hair around her face."

Mrs. Salazar said, "She no here. I never seen her. I never heard of her." She smiled nervously, glanced from me to Dezler with anxious eyes.

Dezler said, "Come on, Kruger, what is this crap?"

"It's because you're here. She's afraid your uniform means Elvia's in trouble, which means she's in trouble if she admits Elvia lives here. Elvia is an illegal and this woman figures you're looking to send her back."

Dezler said, very slow, "Understand lady, I ain't with immigration. No *La Migra*, *verdad*? I could care less if this Reyes chiquita has her card. I write tickets, I guard City Council cars. I don't round up wetbacks."

Mrs. Salazar said again, "I never hear of no Elvia Reyes."

Dezler turned to me. Said, "Let's get outta here. This woman never heard of your broad. I don't consider it a privilege tramping through torn up neighborhoods, talkin' to people who don't talk back, listenin' to a lyin' solo investigator shout questions like he's working a carnival midway." He stomped out the front door.

I removed the three-by-five notebook I carry in my jacket. Wrote on the first blank page: ELVIA, CALL ME. I FOUND RICARDO—KRUGER. Ripped the page free of the spiral rings, handed it to Mrs. Salazar. Said, "I was wrong. Obviously you don't know Elvia Reyes, it must of been somebody else. But on the chance a woman who calls herself Elvia Reyes shows up at this house, give this to her. Will you do that?"

She smiled, nodded. Said, "But I don't know—"

"I know that. But if it *should* happen. Just promise, okay?

She nodded harder.

So by 4:00 P.M. I was back at the office I share with my one good friend, Marvin Torkelson, on North Lincoln Ave, listening to Marvin discuss the Cub's pennant chances. He does this end-lessly every spring before the season starts because after it starts there isn't much to discuss about Cubs pennant chances beyond slim and none. I figured I was finished with Elvia and Ricardo Reyes and the brown paper bag.

That made me sad because Elvia owed me eighty bucks. The deal had been one hundred dollars —twenty up front, eighty when I located Ricardo. Well, I'd located Ricardo. But it ap-peared Elvia had taken a powder, leaving me with a twenty dol-lar bill to show for a day's work. I made better money than that twenty years ago when I was eighteen playing "Louie Louie" at high school sock hops.

At 4:15, a man walked into the office, asked which one of us was Dan Kruger. Marvin wasn't so he excused himself and headed for the pizza parlor next door.

It was the first week in April, cool and wet-smelling outside, but the man wore no jacket. Just a pale blue, short-sleeved shirt, open at the collar, tucked into navy gabardine pants. He looked to be in his fifties. He had an expressionless face and a shaggy swatch of steel gray hair that ran around the sides of his head starting above Dumbo ears. Liver spots freckled his high fore-head. He wore square-framed glasses. His arms were thin and hairless and the puny muscles under his taupe-colored skin looked soft as butter.

He sat down in the chair at the side of my desk. Said, "My name is Orlando Finney." He inserted an unfiltered Lucky Strike into a plastic holder, put it to his lips and lit up. He re-sumed talking while exhaling smoke. "I'm looking for Ricardo Reyes. So are you. I'll pay you one hundred dollars if you tell me where he is instead of his sister."

"She already gave me a hundred," I lied.

"Then I'll make it two hundred." He spoke in an offhand, urbane manner and his gestures were womanly—tender, linger-ing. He held the cigarette to his mouth too long, tilted his head just so and exhaled slow and leisurely from rounded lips, then held the cigarette in front of him and cocked his head like he was posing for an Esquire fashion ad.

"Why all the interest in Ricardo Reyes all of a sudden?"

"Because all of a sudden he vanished."

"How'd you know Elvia hired me?"

He waved his hand with the cigarette in it, said nothing.

I said, "I don't bargain unless I know those things."

"He worked for me, he stole some things from me. I need them back."

"Call the police."

He smiled like he was used to dealing with the mentally deficient. Said, "It's not like I demand a green card when I hand out job applications. I'm afraid the police would suggest I go scratch my ass after reminding me that it is against the law to hire wetbacks."

"What line of work you in?"

"That is no concern of yours. We don't need to make this too complicated, do we?"

"Again, how'd you find out Elvia hired me to look for him?"

"I guessed, good enough?"

"No."

"Find him yet?"

"Maybe."

"Elvia gave you at least one lead, didn't she? Maybe more than one?"

"Maybe a dozen."

He narrowed his eyes, nodded. "You found him already. Does Elvia know?"

I shrugged, tried to look modest.

"Mr. Kruger, it is imperative I find Ricardo Reyes and I don't have time to sit here and fence with you. No time for cat and mouse, understand? I'll give you two hundred fifty dollars if you tell me where he is."

"Show me the money, Finney."

He reached behind him for his wallet, took out two hundreds, one fifty, pushed them at me across the desk. As he did he said, "Straight goods, Mr. Kruger. I'd have to resort to violence if you jerk me around and you wouldn't enjoy that, I'm sure."

"That's a threat, Finney. Technically you just broke a law, but I have a feeling that's not a novelty or of great concern to you. No, this is legit. He's at 2121 West Harrison and Elvia doesn't know yet because now I can't find Elvia. You leave now, you're a lock to beat her to him."

He left hurriedly. I was much happier now. I had two hundred fifty dollars cash, which I could stuff in my wallet without the government knowing I ever owned it, plus I'd learned a little about Mr. Orlando Finney. Like he wasn't much of a Chicagoan. 2121 West Harrison is the county morgue.

THREE

I named my rabbit 'Bugs' even though he isn't gray—he's a black and white French Lop, he doesn't say "What's up, Doc?" when he gets introduced, and he spits carrots out like they were mud. Wouldn't eat one if he was starving. But after all those years of watching Loony Tunes, it would seem incorrect somehow to name a bunny anything else.

At 7:00 P.M., I was blasting him his daily marijuana. Every night, I smoke a joint before supper and I sail the last long exhale at Bugs. I don't know if bunnies get high, but every evening, he hops a bee line to the couch soon as he hears the rustle of rolling papers being removed from their pouch. He sits motionless on my lap afterward, twitching his nose while I scratch behind his droopy, bent-in-half ears. And I believe it helps his appetite. He tears into his bunny chow and watercress like a lumberjack.

So my bunny and I were pleasantly detached and content and listening to Buddy Guy play the blues on my boom box when someone hammered on my front door. When I opened it, Elvia Reyes stuck the piece of paper I'd left with Mrs. Salazar under my nose. "Where is Ricardo?" she said instead of hello.

I pointed her to the couch, switched off the tape. Elvia wore acid-washed jeans and an oversized black sweater. Her long blonde-black hair was windsnarled, and after she sat down, she fingercombed it behind her ears.

Bugs hopped behind the metal radiator in front of the window like he always does when he's out of his cage and a stranger enters the house. Pot probably makes bunnies paranoid, too. Elvia smiled quickly when she saw him, then frowned and looked up at me. Repeated, "Where is Ricardo?"

I said, "A man named Orlando Finney is looking for your brother too. Know him?"

"No. Did Ricardo have the bag with him?" Her English was only slightly accented, but she talked fast, stumbling her way past words.

I said, "You were right about Stacey Ford. He sent me straight to Ricardo."

She said very exasperated, "Does Ricardo have the bag?"

"What did you want more, Ricardo or this bag?"

"Tell me."

I sat down next to her, wishing I was straight because of what I had to tell her. She was licking her long lips. In my stoned condition, they looked ear to ear. I said, "Elvia, Ricardo is dead. He was murdered at the Elizabeth Hotel early today."

She blinked several times, whispered something in Spanish to herself, then asked anxiously, "What about the bag? Did they get the bag?"

"Did you hear me? Your brother is dead."

"Ricardo is twelve years older than me. In Mexico when I was a little girl, Ricardo treats me like I am invisible. Like I am dirt. I never talk to him until he come up to Chicago three months ago. He needs me then so he talks to me. Maybe I care, I don't know. All I know for sure is I want that bag."

"What's in it?"

"Something that belongs to me."

"Finney says that too. I don't believe either one of you."

"You working for him or me?"

"I only work for people who pay me."

"I gave you twenty dollars."

"He gave me two hundred and fifty."

"Mercenary," she hissed. "That is the right word, isn't it?"

"Poverty stricken and practical are better ones."

She got a cunning look on her face. She said, "Or did you find the bag? Have you got it?"

"Whoever killed your brother did it to get that bag and that was not me. All I found was Ricardo's body. And what *I'm* getting out of it is a truckload of grief from the cops because Mrs. Salazar lied like hell. Not that I blame her, understand, but they believe she's telling the truth and I'm not. It's bad enough they don't believe me when I con 'em, I expect that. But when I tell the truth and then can't prove it, it makes me appear to be a class A buffoon. Reinforces their basic opinion of me."

"*Zonzo*, I was out the back door as soon as Mrs. Salazar told me a policeman was at the front door. Like I'm going to stay in that house and talk to a policeman without a green card? Green cards cost money and money is something I don't have yet." She stared straight ahead, lit a Winston and blew out a cloud of smoke as she fanned the match dead. She said, "Dammit to hell," and then started bouncing her skinny legs up and down, her elbows bobbing on her knees.

I didn't say anything, waited for her to talk.

She said, "Could you find the bag?"

"You haven't paid me for finding your brother yet."

"Find the bag. Please?" Her voice was soft now, pleading. "Or find who killed Ricardo. It is the same thing."

"You propose I should canvass Chicago looking for one particular paper sack? I don't even know what's inside."

"What is 'canvass'?"

"It means what you want is impossible. You asking me to track down one paper sack is like asking me to find a hair curler or a book of matches."

Still staring at the wall she said, "There was enough money in that bag that I will not have to worry about money ever again."

I said, "On the other hand nothing's impossible. But maybe your brother put the money in a bank."

"Ricardo wouldn't know what to do in a bank except rob it. No, he had it with him."

"How'd he get it?"

"He stole it from me. He wanted to go back to Tocambaro. He came up in December and he hated the ice and snow. He spent all winter complaining about the cold. He wanted to go back home but didn't have any money."

"How'd you get the money?"

"That's not your worry."

"Is the money Orlando Finney's?"

"No." She continued to stare at the wall, her legs still bouncing.

"Who knew Ricardo had the bag besides you? And Orlando Finney."

"Nobody should of."

I stood up. Said, "Hire somebody else and get out of here."

She said, "You have the money, don't you? You have it and now you want to get rid of me."

"You're half right. I wanna get rid of you. Come back if you decide to tell a truth or two. I don't mind a few lies thrown in to make me earn my money, but you've done nothing but lie since you walked in the door. Out."

I had to drag her to and out the door. The whole time she squirmed and kicked and yelled, "Give me my money."

FOUR

Next morning, I stopped by the Monroe Street station house, asked about Orlando Finney. Got a lot of shrugs and "Fuck Orlando Finney" in reply. Then I ran into a Mexican-American rookie named Benavides. He was in his early twenties and was very earnest and anxious to help. That's how I knew he was a rookie. In the crowded foyer, with cops and undesirables bustling around us, I asked him what business Finney was in.

"He said, "The wetback business and probably more."

"Smuggling illegals?"

"Right. He has a taxi service that brings them up here, then he parcels them out to sweatshops and janitorial services and fly-by-night construction outfits who pay one quarter union wage. You've heard the term shadow labor market? That's Finney's gig. He's been running wets for a while now. I remember him back when I was in my teens. He pimped then. He was constantly prowling Pilsen looking for *mojada* Mex girls just up. The less English they knew the better. He's Anglo looking, speaks fluent Spanish, way he looks screams homosexual. He seemed unthreatening to the girls. But it was like the spider and the fly. Got busted pimping so many times he eventually quit. Now he smuggles IA's. With a dude like him setting up rides down there and seeing to jobs at this end, it's lots safer for the *mojadas* than swimming the Grande and walking all that way through the mesquite with the green hats and the rattlesnakes and the redneck thugs waiting for them. This way they pay to get driven straight here and there's usually some kind of job waiting for them when they get here. Course not all of them can afford it, but those that can got a leg up on the rest."

"He make decent money?"

Benavides shrugged. "I would imagine not a whole lot per individual. I don't know the rates. But remember he gets paid on both ends. The wets pay to use the taxi service down south, and both the wets and the employers kick back to him when they get to Chicago and go on the job. It adds up."

"So why's he on the street if you know his whole operation?"

"It's immigration's problem, not ours. We haven't got the time or manpower to be raiding factories, asking wetbacks how did they get here and who got them their job. They wouldn't tell you anyway."

"Is Finney from Mexico?"

"Nope. Born on 26th Street."

"How'd he get so fluent in Spanish?"

"Mother was Cuban I think."

"What was his father?"

"What's Finney? Irish maybe, I don't know."

"Why, if Finney's been in Chicago all his life, would he not know where the morgue is?"

"I couldn't say."

A light went on in my head and I said to myself, "Unless he knows exactly where the morgue is and was hurrying some-where else after I told him the address and he realized Ricardo was dead." To Benavides I said, "You got any idea where Finney lives? Where he hangs out?"

He shrugged. "Try Pilsen."

An hour later, I walked out of my office, Pilsen my destina-tion, running Orlando Finney to ground my goal.

But there Finney was, leaning against the side of my olive green 1974 Skylark parked in the lot in front of our building. He wore a lavender short-sleeved shirt and no jacket again even though it was cooler than the day before and low gray-black clouds promised rain. It was unnerving, Finney waiting for me outside my office door, but Stacey Ford was standing next to him and that went way beyond unnerving.

Finney said, "You going somewhere, Kruger?" He blew cigarette smoke into the air from o-formed lips. His right hand gently smoothed down the chest of his shirt.

I kept my eyes on Ford because he kept his eyes on me. He wore a tattered blue jean jacket, Levis, big-heeled cowboy boots. Oily bangs swooped low over narrowed eyes. His arms were folded across his chest and he tapped his fingers on his biceps. He chewed the insides of his mouth and his countenance was stern.

I said, "I was going to look for you, Finney, but you found me first."

"Give me my stuff, Kruger."

"Don't *you* start."

"Give it."

"Sorry, don't got."

"If not you, who?"

"Offhand I'd guess whoever killed Ricardo Reyes has it because that would've been a grand reason to bump him, but seeing as I didn't kill him, it follows—"

Finney said, "You think I killed him? That why you were looking for me?"

"Only wanted to ask some questions."

"What about?"

"Why were you looking for Reyes? Really."

"I told you my reasons."

"And I still don't believe you. Did you bring Reyes up to Chicago.

"You mean do I smuggle wetbacks? Listen, I don't bring anybody 'up' to Chicago. Where'd you hear this?"

"Just the police department."

Ford started smiling at me. It wasn't an evil smile, but it was no smile of friendship either. So while I listened to Finney lie to me, I kept my eyes on Ford, ready to duck and cover.

Which caused me to be off guard when Finney stepped forward and drove a left into my stomach. He followed that with a right cross to the jaw. I was so unprepared he could've whaled away to his heart's content except that the second punch put me on my ass. All oxygen rushed from my lungs and refused to come back. I sat on the cold cement, head down, arms resting on raised knees, sucking air like a cornered fox.

Finney hunkered down in front of me, resting his butt on his left heel. Above us Ford was laughing and he said, "Hey, Finney, that wasn't hardly kosher, a sucker punch like that." My brain was receiving static noises and I kept sipping air but none of it would go as far as my lungs. I felt that panic you feel when you think you're going to suffocate from having the wind knocked out of you. After some seconds, I got a little air in me and started to calm down. I stared at Finney's smooth, thin arms, amazed. It was hard to believe those pipe cleaner arms could hit that hard.

He said, "I will not play verbal volleyball with you. That's not why I came here today. Kruger, I want that bag. It's mine and I want it back. Forget what anybody else tells you, what Ricardo Reyes had is mine."

I looked into his eyes, was surprised to see fear. Under the present circumstances, I knew he wasn't afraid of me, but he was definitely scared of something. Maybe he was afraid I was telling the truth. To some people—like Finney and Elvia Reyes—I could see where that would constitute such a unique concept it might be scary. He ran his hand unsteadily around his mouth. Said, "I think you got the bag when you found Reyes. At the very least I think you know where it is."

"Don't think so much, Finney, you're no good at it."

Sometime during all this, a cold mist had started. I watched the water make tiny blisters on Finney's arms and face. He swung his head around, looked up at Ford who shrugged, then turned back to me. He said, "Okay, I'll give you twenty-four hours because of the small chance you don't have it. But if that is true and you even suspect you know who does have it, do yourself a favor and start dealing with them. At noon tomorrow, I want what's mine, and if I don't get it, you will sincerely regret you got mixed up in all this."

FIVE

At the Elizabeth Hotel, a middle-aged woman fatter than Kate
Smith sat behind the cage. She wore a lilac jogging suit that did
its best to cover everything. She informed me the sign-in man
was her father and he was upstairs in his apartment. She gave
me the number only after asking a half dozen questions that
added up to why did I want to pester him on his day off.

He answered my knock wearing the Cubs cap, white boxer
underwear, white socks and black wing tip shoes. Nothing else.
Behind him was a room the duplicate of the one I discovered
Ricardo Reyes in. But with more stuff. Heavy black drapes were
drawn shut with the ends pinned together. A black and white
TV set was on, sound off, shining blue-gray light onto a TV din-
ner set in front of it. Lamps on either side of the room provided
meager pools of light. The room reeked of cigarettes, beer, and
marijuana. It was ten to noon but this room had the feel of 2:00
A.M. In the faint light, I could barely make out ragged white piles
that stood everywhere. I looked closer at the nearest one. They
were newspapers. Stacks of *Tribunes*, *Sun-Times*, and *Readers*.
They covered the floor, most of the bed, the top of the dresser,
spilled out of the closet.

The man didn't invite me in. He asked what I wanted. I said
information about Ricardo Reyes.

He made a sour face. "I run the desk, PI. I don't catalog facts
about my guests in my head. Usually they ain't the type of people I want to reflect on in my spare time."

"When'd he rent the room?"

"Cops asked me that."

"Now I am. But it hurts to know I'm only as original as they
are."

"Around nine yesterday morning. But he'd been staying here
off and on for about two weeks. This time he was gone three
days, came back nine yesterday morning."

"Police ask anything else?"

"Police asked me three things: When did he sign in, did anybody visit him, and did anybody hear a commotion coming out of 214 at any time?"

"Your answers?"

"Nine A.M., no, and no."

"I got a ten spot says you can remember better about visitors."

He said, "Gimme the sawbuck. I didn't tell the cops everything because one, I don't like cops, and two, they didn't give a shit anyway as I'm sure you noticed. Goldbricking sons of bitches. And who pays 'em? You and me, pal. What the hell do they care if a wetback gets his neck slit, huh? Hell, what do I care and it happened right above me practically. Send every goddamn one of 'em back to tamale-land. They act like this country is one giant welfare office. Goddamn, they don't belong here, they—"

I shoved ten bucks in his hand. Said, "Cut the flag-waving, pop. I ain't the Marines, remember? Who came in and asked about Reyes before I did?"

"Some Mex kid, wearing his gang colors. I don't know what gang, but he had on a green and gray sweater and a green beret tilted low over his left eye. All kinds of pins and symbols tacked on the beret."

"You sure it was a gang?"

"Well, he mighta been a Boy Scout lookin' to help one of my elderly residents cross Clark Street, but I doubt it."

"There was only one? Gangbangers wouldn't leave their territory wearing colors unless they had a carful."

"Only one came in, Okay? There coulda been a cattle truck full of the bastards outside, but I don't know that because only the one came in. He came in about five minutes after I rented 216 for a day to some fancy dressed, scarred young guy with a briefcase who I figure for a fag who needs a place to get blown. I notice the gang kid right away because he acts super nervous, pacin' back and forth in front of the door before he finally comes in. He asks if Ricardo Reyes is signed in. I tell him sure but it's going to cost because I got problems with one guy rentin' my rooms, letting all his buddies sleep there. That's why I asked you for a sawbuck."

"The kid pay?"

He nodded. "We argue back and forth a couple minutes. We both get hot, then I say I'm callin' the cops. He real quick forks over a fin, I give him the room number."

"What time was this?"

"Maybe an hour before you came."

"How long he stay up there?"

"Not very long. Couple minutes max. He comes back down the stairs two at a time and was out the door."

"He say anything?"

"Not to me."

"He carrying anything?"

"Like what?"

"A bag?"

"Not that I saw."

"Maybe he had something bulky stuffed under his sweater."

"I didn't frisk the little son of a bitch. Just so he was gone, that was all I cared about."

"You also lie to the police about anybody hearing noises from the room?"

"Nope. Nobody said nothin' to me about hearing anything. But I guarantee if anybody did they wouldn't be talking for public consumption. My clientele may not be upwardly mobile but they know when to shut the fuck up."

"It bother you you could've probably fingered Reyes' killer?"

He barked a laugh. "Hell, no. I told you I don't like wetbacks and on top of that I don't like cops, so why would I go outta my way to help out either category? And why would I wanna get some vicious spic gang ticked off at me? So I didn't say nothin' and I promise you this, my friend, you run to the law and start shooting off your mouth, I'll call you a liar to your face, then sue you for defamation of character."

I smiled, said, "Why tell me then?"

"You gave me ten bucks. And you got to hustle up a living. There's always something for cops to do, plus they got a guaranteed salary."

"Anybody else stop by asking questions yesterday?"

"Late afternoon, a punk I used to see with Reyes sometimes.

Mean looking, skinny kid with blond hair."

"You tell him what you just told me?"

"Some of it. Cost him twenty bucks."

"Thanks for the blue light special." Before I turned to leave I said, "I gotta ask, guy. What's with the papers?"

He went, "Huh?" and looked behind him, then back at me. Said defensively, "I collect 'em, that okay with you? Besides I feel more comfortable reading about world crisis and stuff if I know it ain't a crisis no more. Bad news don't worry you so much when you read it a month after it happens and you know everything's cooled down."

I had to admit it made sense.

SIX

I was sure green and gray meant the Romeo Kings. Pronounced Ro-may-o, the Kings were a Mexican street gang. They weren't the largest or the smallest or the meanest gang in Chicago. Just one of many. The thought of dickering and dealing with them for anything they had, especially a sack of Dead Presidents, was ludicrous. But what the hell.

I ran background checks once for a Latino who could fill in some details. His name was Luis Santiago. He directed Pilsen community action groups, including one called the Hispanic Alliance for Community Development through Voter Strength, which operated out of a small brick building on 19th. I remembered Santiago fondly because the night he paid me for my investigation of two Alliance board members, we closed a Spanish bar on Blue Island. That night, he kept telling me gringo money was no good in bars on Blue Island, which made him a prince in my book. He also told me that night about his younger brother who'd started hanging with the Romeo Kings because he felt ostracized from society and needed to "belong." Luis had nipped that in the bud and shipped his brother to a grandmother in Mexico City before he ended up in jail or the morgue. That had been two years ago. Santiago had spent the better part of an hour that night railing against Latino street gangs. Part of his job was trying to convince gangbangers to leave their gang and become productive community members. His success rate was not high.

We met for a late lunch at Nuevo Leòn on West 18th. Molletes, cactus salad, and Mexican beer. Me feeling like the alien because of the Spanish language posters and signs on the wall and because of all the Spanish voices around me.

Santiago was dressed in a pinstriped gray suit with a white shirt and a burgundy tie. His thick black hair was blow-dried into a high pompadour. Slender fingers constantly stroked a bushy mustache. His skin was a striking shade of beige, a pale peach almost. His most impressive and attractive feature was his smile. It was genuine, friendly and revealed square, snow white teeth that gleamed like polished porcelain. He realized how good he looked when he smiled; he did it often. It disarmed those he spoke to and it caused him to look boyishly charming on television. I had been seeing him occasionally the last year or so on the ten o'clock news and Sunday morning talk shows. The smile made what he had to say seem not so hostile or controversial, which it wasn't of course. All he ever said, basically, was 'Give my people a fucking break.'

But he was saying it on TV now. I guess that made him a Hispanic spokesman.

He told me I was correct. Green and gray meant Romeo King. He told me that, then watched with a grave expression as I took a long drink of beer. Smile or no smile, here was another sincere, earnest Mexican man, this one in his thirties, willing to play the game by the Anglo's rules, even though he knew the Anglo always rigged the game. Thinking he could somehow unrig it through the system. Santiago could've been Benavides older brother.

I said, "They into any new activities?"

"If it's illegal, I imagine they are."

"Besides heroin and coke?"

"Sure. Ups, downs, pot, pills, name it. You looking to score?"

"Nah, I try to clean up once in awhile. I mean, are they dealing people?"

"People? Illegals?" He pulled on his mustache, stared down at his plate of rice. "I haven't heard that but they could be."

"Reason I ask is, it's possible—not for sure, but possible—that they're tied into the murder of an illegal at the Elizabeth Hotel yesterday."

"Who?"

"Ricardo Reyes. Officially, it's no big deal. I saw one paragraph about it in the *Sun-Times* this morning, and the police act like it was a smash and grab or something."

Santiago nodded.

I said, "Also tied in with the murder is a half-Cuban named Orlando Finney. I learned today his latest in a long line of money-making schemes is running illegals up from the border. The illegals pay him down there, the employers pay him up here. Know anything about that?"

"No. But I know Orlando Finney so what you say doesn't surprise me. I've been trying to run him out of Pilsen for ten years. About five years ago he got shipped to Joliet for assault and battery, which his lawyer copped down from attempted murder. Beat the bejesus out of one of his girls for calling him a half-breed when he was drunk. I thought we had him that time, but he was walking the streets inside a year."

"He punched me out this morning. Surprised hell out of me. Guy looks like a feeble old queen."

Santiago's face got even more serious. "Don't underestimate him, and don't make fun of him to his face. He's not feeble and he's not gay. He's got a terrible temper. A bad news type guy."

"Now he tells me." I lit a Kool, washed some smoke down with beer.

Santiago said, "Why are you involved in all this?"

"Ricardo Reyes' sister hired me to find him. Now Finney thinks I have something that belongs to him."

"Do you?"

"No. So where can I find some of these Romeo Kings?"

He stared at me for a couple of seconds like I was joking. "God, Dan, why?"

"I got questions they can answer. Maybe."

"Well, you could cruise up and down Blue Island looking for green and gray, but they usually hang in packs and you sure don't want to go up alone to a group of them on the street. Tell you what, I'll set up a meeting. At the building, we got rooms, there'll be people around. You can ask questions and not worry you're going to get a blade or a brick for an answer. There's a lot of bitterness against Anglos on the street."

"I got no quarrel and I don't plan to finger anybody, I just want information."

"I realize that, but—hell, I understand why they're so bitter. It's bleak around here. People are angry. Poverty is a crushing type of condition. It produces no hope, no future." He leaned forward, into his spiel, like he was on Sunday Morning Newsmakers. "Street fiestas and wall murals only go so far. A man can endure anything if you give him hope, but you yank that away and he has nothing. That's why I plead with them to register to vote. So Hispanics can become a united power block and we can get a say in what goes on. Like the blacks did with Washington."

"Anybody listen?"

"Some. Most of the under thirties are too cynical. They see their mothers working in sweatshops downtown for minimum wage and they say the hell with that. My other problem is half the older Mexicans up here plan on returning to Mexico soon as they save up some money. Then they can start up a store or buy a small farm. They're *Mexican*, you see, and they consider being here a working vacation. They think becoming a United States citizen and registering to vote is unpatriotic to Mexico. For most of them this dream will never happen; they're going to stay here, they're going to die here, but you can't tell them that. Some don't become citizens because of the ancient stories that say they have to sell any land they own in Mexico, or they have to stomp on the Mexican flag in front of a judge. Some people still believe that."

I lit another Kool, checked the clock on the wall, but Luis wasn't done yet.

He said, "And then there's the factions to deal with. Mex versus P.R., P.R. versus Central Americans and on and on. The pecking order changes with the nationality. It's nuts. Makes things damn difficult." He paused, sipped some beer, his eyes looking beyond me. "And the *indocumentados*. They can't register for anything. They're too busy looking over their shoulders for *La Migra* and getting ripped off by Mexican con men who tell them they can purchase a green card for two hundred dollars. Many people fall for that scam. Of course, they never see cards or their money again."

Just for talk I said, "Must be a bitch."

Santiago stared at me like he'd forgotten I was there. He beamed his dazzling smile. Said, "Ah, listen to me. Like you asked about all this stuff. What the hell, I got a lifetime, right?"

When I left, I asked him to set up the meeting soon. He said to call back the next morning.

SEVEN

I shouldn't have been surprised, but I was, when I got back to the office to find three Romeo Kings waiting for me. One in my visitor chair, one in my own chair, one in Marvin's chair pulled in front of my desk. Marvin sat on the corner of his desk, holding a Midwestern Insurance Company brochure in front of him like he was reading it. He strived to appear at ease, but pulled it off with all the élan of a three-legged antelope getting shoved into a lion's cage.

When I walked past him, he muttered fast, "I'll get you for this, Kruger. I swear to God I will."

It would've been dangerous for a Romeo King to travel so far north through so many enemy territories in full battle regalia so the three wore plain green windbreakers, gray Levis, and lime green high-top sneakers.

The kid in my chair had a boot camp buzz cut and a face full of acne. The face also had at least a dozen long knife scars. Like he'd been held down while someone carved his cheeks and chin at their leisure. The swerving dead white lines and the patches of red acne between them made his face look like a grotesque

road map of a mountainous region. He stared up at me, daring me to comment. He looked like a future lifer, so of course I didn't, but it was my chair and I had to say something about that. I couldn't afford to start a relationship with people like this exhibiting fear. I said, "Out of the chair, sport."

The look in his eyes changed to confusion. He said, "But if I get up, where do I sit?"

"I don't really care."

"I ain't sittin' on the floor, man."

I nodded at his two buddies. "They got laps."

He still didn't move. I tilted the chair forward, back, forward, back. Said, "Get out or fall out, it's all the same to me."

He stood up quickly, walked around the desk and stood behind Marvin's chair. He said, "You wouldn't do that in my house."

"I suppose not."

The guy in Marvin's chair was six foot plus and very fat with a shaved head and a scraggly mustache. The third King, the one in my visitor chair, was a cleancut shrimp—about five-two, one hundred pounds—with a baby face that made him look like a junior high honor student. He kept staring in my direction, but he wore mirror sunglasses so I couldn't tell if he was looking at me.

The very fat King grinned broadly, looked ready to growl, "We don't need no stinking badges." He was older than the other two, mid-twenties to their late teens, and from the way map face stood behind him, I took him for the leader. I said to him, "Why does the short person stare at me?"

He said, "Garcia? He's only dreamin', man, that's all. Not starin', dreamin'. You're hip to dreamin', aren't you?"

As he said that, the cleancut shrimp's head tilted sideways, then slowly fell forward like he was bowing. He breathed shallow and quick, then snorted loudly. The two awake Kings belly-laughed. The one standing said, "*Ando Sonado.* Hey, let's give Garcia the finger. He won't know it." They both started flipping off Garcia, laughing uncontrollably.

Marvin dropped the brochure and walked out the door. While the boys had their fun, I took out my Valium bottle from the desk drawer and swallowed two without water. Then I lit a Kool and waited.

They stopped when Garcia's upper torso came to rest on his thighs.

The fat King said, "Garcia is a rabbit. You hip to what a rabbit is?"

I said, "Yeah." A rabbit is a drug tester. Like the canaries in coal mines.

He laughed. "I'd say we got some dynamite dope, wouldn't you?"

I said, "The rabbit better not throw up on the floor."

The very fat King said, "What would you do if he does?"

"Watching him might make me sick. I might throw up on you."

"I don't think so."

I shrugged. "I could be wrong."

He said, "My name is Enrique Medina, but you can call me Ricky, most Anglos do. Where is Orlando Finney?"

"Don't know. Best I can do is tell you where he'll be noon tomorrow."

"Where?"

"Here, or wherever he tracks me down. He hangs out in your neighborhood from what I hear. You should be able to locate him no problem."

"He went basement on us. Nobody's got any idea where he is. You workin' for him?"

"No. You sure you want Orlando Finney?"

"No, man, I ask the question because of how much I love the sound of my voice. It's why we're here."

I said, "I don't think you want Finney. I think you want a paper bag."

"I don't know nothin' about no bag. I want Finney."

"Half of Chicago wants that bag." I was pretty sure now I knew what Finney was afraid of. Wanting to know why I said, "Tell me why you want him so bad?"

"Personal matter."

"Why come here looking for him?"

"We got us a tip."

"Who from?"

"Anonymous tip. You see, we operate like the law. We don't give out information like that. You keep things confidential, you keep your friends, you keep your contacts."

"Which one of your boys wanted to see Ricardo Reyes?"

"I don't know what you're talking about."

"Elizabeth Hotel? Yesterday? A Romeo King went inside, asked for Reyes, went upstairs, ran back down in a big hurry. I come by an hour later, go upstairs, find Reyes dead, his throat grinning at me. And except for the gallons of blood on the floor, the room is clean as a whistle. Everything he owned gone. Including a brown shopping bag that everybody I meet now wants and thinks I must have. But you act like you know I don't have it. You knew Ricardo Reyes, right?"

"I know a shitload of Reyeses. Every Mexican that ain't named Martinez, Gonzalez or Garcia is named Reyes. But I don't know no Ricardo Reyes who is now dead. The police know about the King goin' up and down the stairs?"

"The deskman at the Elizabeth has too much respect for you gentlemen to be telling stories like that to a uniform."

Medina smiled wide. "Respect is an admirable trait to possess. You treat a King with respect, he returns the favor."

"Just like Aretha Franklin."

"Funny. But seriously, I'd hate to see the Kings become mixed up in something we are innocent of. I think any person who hears that story about the King on the stairs should remember to have respect for us."

I said, "Luis Santiago was supposed to arrange me a meeting with you guys. You talk to him before you came here?"

"Fuck Luis Santiago and the burro he rode here on. He don't talk to us about nothin', and we don't talk about nothin' to him. Listen up, amigo. When you see Orlando Finney, you tell him Enrique Medina and the Romeo Kings desire a conversation with him. Urgently." He stood up.

I said, "What's in this for me?"

Ignoring me, the two conscious Kings hefted their cleancut junkie friend from the chair, one on each side, and carried him to the door, his feet dangling a foot above the floor.

They stopped at the door, and over his shoulder Medina said, "And remember, Kruger, that's R-E-S-P-E-C-T."

EIGHT

My apartment is the first floor of a two-story house covered with imitation gray brick. It's two blocks east of Wrigley Field. I'm a White Sox fan—a rare North Side animal—so Wrigley was not a prime selling point when I signed my lease, but it's there and all summer I have to put up with it.

The day after the three Romeo Kings visited me was Cubs opening day. The Mets. The Cubs looked to be mediocre again; what else was new? But Cub fans don't care, they'll watch anything. Upholding Chicago's opening day tradition, the morning was raw and blustery, more fitting for a Bears game than baseball. At 11:30, I cradled Bugs and we looked out the front window, watching groups of happy Cub fans trot towards the ball park. The smart ones, the ones who've been in Wrigley anytime before July first, were wrapped and scarfed like Alpine skiers. You can spot the burbies or the casual opening day fan who don't realize Wrigley is only a couple of blocks from the Lake. They wear windbreakers or light sweaters like they're on their way to watch a summer sport.

As we watched, I talked to my bunny because he's such a good listener. Must be the ears. I said, "What the hell goes on, eh Bugs? Finney's gonna come visiting today, wanting that damn bag, and I haven't got a single thing to tell him. Obviously, Elvia stole that bag from somebody, probably Finney, but how'd she get her hands on it? What was the money for? If it *is* money. There's always the chance she lied about that too. Why was it only in a paper sack? Who has it now? My money's on the Kings, but why are they so interested in Finney if they've already got the bag?" I paused. "Bugs, speak to me."

I turned Bugs over, crossed my arms under his back; he stared up at me, twitched his nose, blinked. I blew onto his belly. Bugs enjoys that.

"Ah, Bugs, you say what difference does it make? Nobody's paying me now so why should I care, right? It's like this you

scwewy wabbit, I'm involved whether I got a boss or not because everybody believes I have the bag. They think that when I found Reyes, I found the bag. Course now, somebody out there knows that ain't true, but too many people believe it is and they are going to be persecuting the hell out of me."

I looked from Bugs to outside. Said, "And here comes one of them now."

Crossing Fremont, behind a battalion of fans, Stacey Ford swaggered, staring at me in the window. His hands were jammed in his jeans pockets, his Levi jacket was open, his bangs lifted and settled as he walked.

I opened the door before he rang the bell. He stared at Bugs and said, "That's a goddamn rabbit."

"You're a perceptive man, Ford. Finney send you here for the bag?"

"Yeah."

"I haven't got it. I think I know who does, but if he wants to take it from them, he can be my guest."

"So what? Fuck Finney."

"You aren't partners?"

"Yeah, but fuck him anyway. Come on, I got a friend wants to meet you."

"Who?"

"Just a guy. It's not a set up. Just a meeting."

"Sure it's not Finney?"

"Not Finney."

I scooted Bugs back in his cage, put on my black windbreaker, shoved a pack of Kools and a bottle of Valium in the pocket.

Ford's car was double-parked two blocks over on Broadway. He drove a yellow, ten-year-old Chevy. Well, originally it was yellow; the side panels were almost solid rust now. We got on Lake Shore Drive going south toward the Loop. Traffic was light and he drove fast, sucking on a Winston and punching radio buttons. Ford was a maniac radio button pusher. Jumped station to station every ten seconds, never paying attention to what came on. He rested his cigarette hand on the selection control tray and the routine was push button, take a drag, push button. When he'd gone from left to right on the dial, he returned right to left.

After awhile I said, "You sore about the other day in the bar?"

He scowled, combed the free fingers of his cigarette hand through his bangs, put the hand back on the radio. Said, "Well, first of all you half-ass apologized while you did it, and I know what it's like takin' on somebody you know can clean your clock. I mean, Mike Tyson is the only man in the world who has the luxury of knowing he ain't gonna meet up with some dude who might kick his ass. And Finney punched you good yesterday. I got a kick out of that. Caught you off guard, didn't he? Frail lookin' old fart punching like that." He flicked the Winston out the window, pushed a button, looked at me. "But, I woulda fucking told you where Reyes was if you asked me. All you had to do was ask. I didn't know what he had with him. If I'd known that, I wouldn'ta told you, but I didn't, so I woulda said 'Elizabeth Hotel' and all it woulda cost you was a beer. And you wouldn't of had to come on like Macho Man Savage."

"Elvia told me I'd have to force it out of you."

"Come on, what was it to me where her brother was? Course you embarrassed me in front of all those people in that bar. That's my regular hangout, too. I practically live here. We ever meet in there again I'll have to tear your ass up to maintain respect."

"Don't worry about it. It's not my type of joint."

"And should you ever see me on the street when I'm slop-ass drunk, run do not walk in the opposite direction. Little things like remembering I got worked over aggravate me when I'm very drunk."

"What was in the bag?"

"Didn't Elvia tell you?"

"She says money, lots of it."

Ford shrugged. "Then money it is. She should know, Ricardo stole it from her."

"Who'd she steal it from?"

"Finney says Finney."

"How'd Finney get it?"

Ford said, "I don't know."

"How long did you know Ricardo Reyes?"

"Not long. This winter I met him."

"How?"

"We did some jobs together."

"What jobs?"

"Just jobs. *Sabe usted hablar Español?*"

"What?"

"Never mind."

"What'd you say?"

"I asked if you talked spic. You answered me when you said 'what?'. I thought because Elvia Reyes hired you maybe you talked the lingo."

"Elvia Reyes hired me because I'm cheap. Where'd you learn Spanish?"

"I lived in Colombia for over a year. Course I don't talk it like a native, but what I picked up gets me by okay. Opened lots of doors for me up here. This town's gonna be Mexico City North in a couple years. I'm gonna be ready."

"Good idea."

Ford said, "Plus I appreciate the culture. Most whites don't, but I like it. It's got romance, mystery I guess. And the women are submissive and passionate and the men rule the roost. You can't beat a set up like that."

"Not with a stick."

Ford went on, "I enjoy studying things, like language and culture and history." He looked sideways at me to see if I'd laugh at him, then said, "You know, bettering my mind? I don't retain things real well though. I don't read good and I have to read things over and over to remember."

"It's the drugs," I said. Lots of people our age have that problem."

"You think so?"

"Sure."

He hit a button, paused for a second. "Look in the glove box."

I opened it. Inside was a dog-eared paperback copy of *The Grapes of Wrath*. I took it out and thumbed through it.

Ford said, "That's what I'm reading now. Got it for ten cents at a church sale. My folks come from Oklahoma so it's real interesting to me. But it's slow going. I'm on page twenty-three, but I've reread the first twenty-two pages about six times."

I said, "Henry Fonda was real good in the movie," and put the book back. "You must of been in the dope business to stay in Colombia for over a year."

He smiled. "You got it."

"Colombia must be a pretty good place to be if you're into drugs."

"Pretty good? It's heaven. The smoke down there, Jesus, a jumbo jet could crash in your backyard, you wouldn't even notice it because you always got that squealing, crashing sound in hour head, you know? And down there cocaine is cheaper than muscatel. The farmers pluck coca leaves right off the plants, chew on it all day. I mean, it's all *over* the place."

"So how come you ain't rich?"

"I worked for somebody else. Guys like me don't get rich."

"We are two of a kind, Ford. You know Elvia Reyes very well?"

Ford punched a button, looked at me and did a Groucho Marx leer.

"She still on 17th in Mrs. Salazar's house?"

"I suppose. I was only there once at night. I went down with Ricardo."

"Where's Finney?"

Ford chuckled. "Hidin'."

"He's really scared of the Kings, isn't he?"

"How'd you know what he's scared of?"

"Three of 'em showed at my office yesterday looking for him."

"Finney is scared of a lot of people," Ford said. He hit three buttons bam-bam-bam.

NINE

Ford maneuvered through the Loop, parked in a lot on Wabash, the one under the Pago Pago painted wall ad. We walked north a couple blocks, then jaywalked under the L tracks while a train thundered overhead. Ford used a key to let us into the front door of a black-windowed club called the Midnight Lounge. I knew at one time the Midnight Lounge had been a full frontal joint, but most of those were in the suburbs now.

Inside was night dark and smelled like old beer and cheap perfume. There was a long polished bar on the right and a room full of round tables stacked with chairs. On the end of the bar was a portable black and white TV with the Cubs game on. Harry Caray was growling about something.

Two Hispanic men mopped the floor, slopping water from plastic buckets. They didn't look at us. At the far end of the club, beyond all the tables and chairs, was a raised, pink-lit bandstand. I'd spent ten years of my life eking out a living with my Gibson guitar on bandstands just like this one so I felt a bit nostalgic as I looked at it. At the back of the stand, a man sat behind a sparkle silver drum set. He was no drummer: He repeatedly wacked the snare and tom-tom like a child galloping short pencils on a table.

We walked carefully across the slippery tile floor to the bandstand. Even under the pale pink light the man's skin looked pale and doughy, like if you pressed him with your finger the indentation would remain. He was running to fat on the sides and stomach, but his chest and shoulders were massive, his biceps enormous. He had a fighter's razor-lined, puffy face with greasy black hair combed high in front like a 1956 punk. He wore a checkered shirt with only the bottom two buttons buttoned. He ignored us at first and kept rolling the drumsticks from tom to snare. Ford sat down on the stand. I lit a Kool, stood and watched.

When the man stopped, he looked me up and down. Said, "You Kruger?"

I nodded.

"I heard your name before. You used to be a guitar player, right? I'm an amateur musician myself."

I said, "I'd say so. I hope you own this club and aren't auditioning for house drummer."

"You sayin' I stink?" His voice was a high, pleasant tenor. From his looks I had pegged his age mid-forties, but the voice sounded like a teen-agers before puberty.

"I could probably word it a little more tactful."

He flipped the sticks in the air. They descended and bounced on the velvet carpet stage. He said, "But why bother, right?" He nodded at the TV across the room on the bar. "How you like the Cubs this year?"

"Same as every year. Hope they go zero and 162."

He grimaced. Muttered, "Sox fan," the way one might say "child molester." Then his face cleared and he said, "You know, this is the damndest thing. I was telling Stacey here just this morning that I needed somebody to find a lost guy for me and he says he just yesterday met somebody who's aces at locating lost guys."

"Life is rich with coincidence."

"And then I tell him the person I need to find is Orlando Finney and he says 'You won't believe this, but the investigator is already involved on a case that Orlando Finney figures prominently in.'"

"It is a small world."

"Stacey also tells me Finney is prepared to get his hands on some money. And it's not such a small world when people decide to drop out of sight, and Stacey tells me that's what Orlando Finney plans to do. Seems he's scared of something. Find him for me."

"We have a problem right off. Finney thinks I'm gonna find that money for him. He's wrong, but that's what he thinks."

"That's no problem."

"Why do you want him?"

"He owes me money. But if he drops out of sight with that money, I'm cooked."

"You can't do any better than me?"

"Meaning?"

"I'm just a small-time private cop. You don't have people you can put on a job like this?"

"You been watchin' too many 'Starsky and Hutch' reruns, Kruger. It's only on TV that nightclub owners got underlings sittin' around ready to carve up people when they give the word. It'd be nice, but—" He leaned back, crossed his arms across his chest and laughed. His laugh was like a little girl's.

I looked at Ford. "Finney sent you to see me today. You should know where he's at."

"Nope. It ain't like he and I are compadres. I just work for him now and then. Yesterday, he found me at my bar and gave me twenty bucks to come with him to see you. He called me last night. He's supposed to call again tonight. If you had the bag, he was gonna set up a meeting, but you don't so I probably won't see him again. He plans to stay underground. Soon as he gets some cash, he's out of here, which is why this man needs to find him fast."

I said, "There you go. Tell him you got the bag and wait for him to show up to get it."

Ford shook his head. "Won't work. Finney ain't stupid. He'd concoct some complicated drop like it was a kidnap case. He'd have me leave the bag off in the Arie Crown lobby after the show's over or in the Water Tower elevator. Someplace where a crowd could cover him or somebody he sent."

"I can't imagine why he doesn't trust you."

"The hell with Finney. He knows I can't stand him."

"Then why'd he send you for the bag? He's not afraid you'll skip with it?"

"Shows how few friends he's got. Besides, he can find me easy enough. It's him nobody can find."

"Why don't he come himself?"

"He's afraid the Kings are tailing you."

"They could tail you too."

"He figures I'd lose them. He doesn't know what you'd do or maybe you wouldn't care one way or the other."

I turned to the drummer. "I don't know your name or your price."

"Joseph Cantel. I'll pay your standard rate."

"My standard rate fluctuates according to the finances of the person hiring me. How much is Finney into you for?"

"None of your business."

I said to no one in particular. "You see what I put up with? Nobody ever wants to tell me shit, but they expect me to jump at the chance to work for 'em."

Cantel said, "You want the job or not?"

"Gotta see some scratch first."

"What you got in mind?"

"I was thinking a hundred down and percentage of what Finney owes."

"How about 500 you find him today, 400 tomorrow and so on? Like an incentive contract."

"I might not find him until next week and end up owing you money."

"Make it 250, flat fee."

I said, "Half up front." As Cantel pulled out his wallet, I said, "What's the plan once I locate Finney? I won't finger him so you can bump him off."

"Come on, think straight. If I was to kill somebody, I wouldn't be hiring strangers to track the victim down. For all I know you got an uncle in the State Attorney's office. If I kill him, I hafta kill you and Ford because you could testify versus me. Then I'd have to kill anybody you told and then anybody they told and on and on. Too heavy for me. I don't think I'd enjoy prison, Kruger. Besides, dead men don't pay their debts and all I want is my money."

Later, Ford and I were back on the Drive, he puffing and punching buttons, me staring at the Lake. Around Chicago Ave., he said, "So what do you think of Cantel?"

"I'm gonna avoid thinking of him as much as possible. I still think you know where Finney is."

Ford shook his head. "If I did I'd have the money you got in your pocket in mine."

"You were with him yesterday."

"Like I told you, he can find me, not vice versa."

"Who you work for, Cantel or Finney?"

"Both."

"Meaning Stacey Ford."

"When you haven't got lots of smarts and you can't retain what you read so well, you learn to hustle like hell and latch on to the people who got the smarts."

I said, "If Finney and Cantel are your idea of people with smarts, you are in bigger trouble than you know."

TEN

After Ford dropped me at my apartment, I drank a quart of Strohs and listened to Otis Rush's *So Many Roads* album to kill some time and let Ford get where I figured he was going. Then I put Bugs in his traveling cage, carried him to the Skylark and we drove to the bar where I'd pulled Ford off the stool.

The bar was called The Dangerous Game. Someday I'd have to find out why. It was on North Milwaukee. I couldn't go inside to see if Ford was there for two reasons, so I cruised side streets and stopped at the mouth of alleys and in front of parking lots, scanning rows of cars. Finally I found Ford's Chevy parked three blocks west of Milwaukee on Altgeld.

I drove past it, used the mid block alley to reverse direction and squeezed into a spot near the alley. The Chevy was half a block in front of me on the other side of the street. I slid the seat back, slouched down, pressed on the Cubs game. They were winning so I punched it off. I lit a Kool.

Bugs was barely awake, stretched long, ears laid back, schnoz twitching. I said to him, "Bugs, I trust Stacey Ford about as much as clover trusts sheep. For all his talk about having no smarts and having to suck up to people who do, Stacey Ford believes he is one smart cookie. And I don't think he thinks that way about me. To use a comparison you'll understand, he thinks he's Bugs Bunny and I'm Elmer Fudd." Bugs closed his eyes. I said, "Wabbit, I can't take you anywhere."

Ford was turning up all over the place and that made me

want to learn something about him, like where he spent the part
of his life he didn't spend stool sitting in The Dangerous Game,
making full glasses empty. To learn that, I was prepared to sit
and wait all afternoon.

That's about what it took. Within one hour, I was out of Kools
because I chain smoke when I'm bored. I ate two Valiums to
calm the nicotine D.T.'s. The Valiums and watching Bugs nap
made me sleepy. I dozed off twice, waking with a start both
times, afraid the Chevy would not be there. It was both times. I
expected to see a squad car real soon. Dozing against the window, I must've resembled your typical junkie on a midday nod,
who might attempt a B&E if I could get myself sufficiently alert
to get out of the car. But none came.

At 4:30, I jerked awake just as the Chevy pulled toward me. I
ducked, turned around in the alley. I followed Ford as he got
back on Milwaukee, up to Diversey where he went left. We
drove twenty blocks on Diversey. At Parkside, he turned left.
Went four blocks, stopped in front of a three story brownstone. I
drove past, shielding my face with my hand. Pulled to the curb a
block up, adjusted the rear view so I could watch. Within fifteen
seconds, Orlando Finney, wearing a short-sleeved white shirt,
black pants, and mirror sunglasses, almost ran from the door of
the brownstone to the passenger door of Ford's car.

Ford thought he was even smarter than I thought he thought
he was.

As they passed, I laid down on the seat, my head on Bug's
cage. I followed again, thinking Ford had to be totally unaware if
he couldn't spot the Skylark on this residential street with little
other traffic.

He turned east, then north on Lincoln. We were eight blocks
from my office before it dawned on me that's where we were
headed. I mumbled, "Way to go, Dan." I'm laughing at Ford for
not noticing my car while he leads me to my own office. But it
was an honest mistake if you looked at it from a rational point of
view. Ford was selling his boss down the river. He had recom-
mended me to helm the boat. And now he was accompanying
his boss—the boatee—to see me—the boater. Either he expected I wouldn't be at the office or assumed I wouldn't say
anything. And the only reason I could think that he'd believe the

latter was if Cantel was the guy Ford was taking to the cleaners. If that was the case, I had a ton of work to do.

They pulled into the parking lot in front of the cinderblock and plate glass building that houses Rocco's Pizza Palace, Elvira's Beauty Shoppe, and Marvin Torkelson's Midwestern Insurance Company office, of which I am one corner.

I double-parked, flashers blinking, half a block shy of the lot.

Ford was going to stay in the car. Okay, finally something made sense here. He *didn't* want me to see them together. Finney opened the passenger door and had one leg out when I heard shouting in Spanish from up the street. Ford started reversing the Chevy with the pedal on the floor before Finney shut the door.

A silver Dodge made a left from the next street north and streaked toward the lot entrance, wanting to seal it off. Ford did a turnaround, tires squealing, and gunned the Chevy onto Lincoln, using half the sloping lot entrance. The right half of the Chevy underside scraped hard on the curb. The Dodge attempted to ram, missed by a hair. It skidded through where the Chevy had just passed and crunched into the rear end of a parked black Cadillac.

Ford hauled ass south down Lincoln, passing me. I stuck my head out the window and watched him book. He darted in and out of traffic, using both lanes, his hand on the horn the whole time.

The Dodge backed away from the Cadillac, then accelerated south, horn blaring.

Four men were in the Dodge. The driver was the very fat Romeo King, Enrique Medina. His friend with the Rand McNally face rode shotgun. I didn't recognize the two in the back seat.

I slipped it into D, pulled into the lot and parked. Went straight to my desk. That was something I wanted no part of.

ELEVEN

At 8:00 P.M., I was in my kitchen eating an epicurean supper. For me an epicurean supper is when I heat the canned beans and pour the beer in a glass.

As I ate, I reviewed the last three days and tried to get a handle on Stacey Ford. I couldn't figure what he was up to. He was only a low level punk, but he was playing some dangerous games. He gave the impression he knew what he was doing, but if that were so, why did he still operate out of life's basement? A hustler with big balls, which was the impression he gave me today, should either be dead or in the chips by his age.

At 8:30 there was a banging on the front door. Finney and Ford must've lost the Kings. I stubbed my cigarette out in the brown sauce, went down the hallway rehearsing lies to tell Finney.

I opened the door. Elvia Reyes ducked around me before I could say anything. She had on the same jeans and black sweater she'd worn the day before. Her blonde-black hair hung around her face like frayed rope.

She went to the couch and sat down. Said, "I'm here to say I'm sorry and I want us to be partners." She stared at the wall again as she spoke.

"What kind of partners?"

"We will find the money together and I'll give you some."

"Fifty-fifty?"

"Not fifty-fifty, but I'll be generous."

"Fifty-fifty is generous. Less isn't."

She looked at Bugs in his cage and she smiled. Her lips were so long that when she smiled her face seemed to split in half.

I took Bugs out of the cage, carried him to Elvia and sat him on her lap. Said, "He'll squirm a little until he's sure he's safe. Don't let him slip between your legs and fall."

I sat next to her and watched her pet Bugs' head and ears,

calming him. She smiled the whole time. She giggled, said, "You call him Bugs?"

"Original, eh? It was either Bugs or Lop Eared Varmint."

"Where'd you get him?"

"A garbage can."

She looked at me, frowning.

I said, "After last Easter. Pet shop people tell me it happens every year. Parents buy rabbits for their kids, then decide a week later they don't want rabbits for their kids because the kids don't take care of the rabbits. So they toss 'em away like old newspapers. Bugs was in an alley dumpster behind the Hollywood Bar on Racine. I was socializing there one night, went out for some air. I heard noises in the dumpster, looked inside, there was Bugs thrashing around. Scared stiff. When I took him out, his heart was beating like a hummingbird wing. He was about half the size he is now. I bought a book about rabbits and made the cage. Before you knew it, we were like Batman and Robin. He keeps improving, I might give him half partnership in the agency. Put his name on the window card, list him in the phone book. The works."

She continued to pet him. I said, "When you left here last time, you were sure I had the money."

"I don't believe that now."

"Why not?"

"I thought about it. I think about this all the time. What's that called?"

"Obssessed."

"Yep, obssessed."

"What do you believe now?"

"I think Orlando Finney killed my brother and he has the money."

"Finney came to my office that afternoon looking for Ricardo. He wanted to find him as bad as you did."

"Sure, to throw everybody off the track. Avoid suspicions."

I said, "I don't think Finney has the money, but if he does, so what? It's his money according to everybody I talk to."

"It is not his," she said heatedly. "It's mine."

"You could walk out the door with Bugs, that wouldn't make him your rabbit."

"Finney didn't get it honest. He stole it, too."

"Who from?"

"I don't know that, but I know a person doesn't acquire that amount of money honest. Especially not Orlando Finney. He's never acquired ten cents honest."

"How much was in that bag?"

"I didn't get to count it, but it was half full of money and it was not one dollar bills. I had it, it's mine."

"If you wanna reason like that, if whoever steals it last gets to keep it, then whoever stole it from Ricardo owns it."

"No, it's mine."

"You're as stubborn as a two-year-old baby."

Elvia scratched Bugs' ears for a bit, then said, "Mr. Kruger, you suspect you are poor, don't you?"

"I don't suspect it. I know it. All I gotta do is read the papers when the government announces the median income level."

"Where I come from in Mexico, you would be the richest man in town to live in a house like this and own a car and a TV and a stereo. You can't even picture what it's like down there. When I came up seven years ago, I vowed I would somehow become rich or I'd die trying. This is my chance. I'm not stubborn, Mr. Kruger, I am determined. Will you help me?"

"Who do you go to if I say no?"

"Nobody. But I'll search for it just the same. Alone, if I have to."

I leaned against the back of the couch, mulled things over for more than a minute. Elvia shifted so she could stare at me. She flicked her hands over Bugs' backbone like she was brushing dandruff away. It's obscene the way the thought of free money digs into your brain. Everybody has a greed compartment up there and thoughts like the one Elvia Reyes was zapping into my head zoomed toward that compartment with the singlemindedness of an air to air missile seeking heat. Orlando Finney had enough money. The Romeo Kings didn't deserve it. Neither did Ford or Cantel. Who was left? For starters, me. It was ridiculous to believe the bag of money was still floating around town, waiting for someone else to snatch it, but what if it was? It wouldn't hurt to come into a little cash. I just turned thirty-seven. Time to start providing for my future. What there would be of it. I constantly worry about having no money, even though it does no good to dwell on it. When opportunity knocks a poor man can't afford to be overly ethical or let some murky personal code of honor rob him of a secure future.

I said, "You have absolutely no idea how difficult it would be. It's just this side of impossible."

"Nothing is impossible, Mr. Kruger."

"Don't start like Knute Rockne on me. If we're gonna be partners better call me Dan."

"You'll help me?"

"Yes. But I warn you now, if we discover this money started out legal, it goes back to whoever owns it."

Her face split in two as she smiled. She said excitedly, "It won't be that difficult, you'll see. We'll narrow down who knew about the bag, and who could have it, and then we'll get it. You'll see, it won't be as difficult as you fear."

TWELVE

That night a low pressure area sailed through town dragging with it a windstorm that screamed along the side of the house and rammed sudden gusts against the front windows like a freight train colliding with a stalled auto.

The lights kept blinking on and off so I extinguished them and lit ten thick vanilla candles, placed them in a circle on the living room floor. Then Elvia and I sat inside the circle—Bugs tightly held in Elvia's lap so he wouldn't hop over to investigate the flames—and wrote down everything that'd happened from the time her brother had punched her around early Monday morning and ran out of Mrs. Salazar's house with the bag. Then we made a list of everybody who might've known about the bag, before and after the murder. It was a short list: Orlando Finney was at the top of it, followed by Enrique Medina and an unknown number of Romeo Kings, Stacey Ford, Joseph Cantel was a 'maybe,' Dan Kruger, Elvia Reyes.

I said, "It's probably the reason Cantel hired me, but he and Ford wouldn't say that of course. Finney might've told Ford after the murder and Ford told Cantel. Ford claims he knew nothing about it when I was looking for Ricardo."

Elvia said, "You can't believe anything Stacey Ford says."

"I don't know how the Romeo Kings found out unless your brother was tight with one of them."

"I don't know about that," she said. We both flinched as another windblast smacked the windows.

I said, "I wish we knew how Finney got the money and what it was for. That would probably explain a lot of things. The only people we know about are the ones who wanted it after you got it. There could be a list of people long as my arm who had it before Finney and are looking for it now."

Evidently, Elvia hadn't thought of that. She said, "That could be," and looked sad.

"Plus there could be somebody with no connection to any of us. Some lowlife at the Elizabeth Hotel who happened to get inside Ricardo's room, saw the bag and killed to get it. In hotels like that, people kill strangers for a bottle of 20/20. They'd kill their mother and father for that much money."

Elvia said, "I still think Finney has it."

"How'd you get it from him? I told you you'd have to be honest with me. Start with that."

She stared down at Bugs and said, "This is not easy for me to talk about. I was raised very devout, you know? Sunday night, I was at Orlando Finney's apartment. He's not living there now, I've been back five or six times. I told him I'd spend the night. Sometimes he gives me money, leaves it on the table by the front door. It helps out a lot. I'm not a prostitute," she said hurriedly. "I don't hustle on the street, but I was working piece rate on a buttonhole machine downtown and they fix it so an illegal never makes rate because they know we can't complain. Finney fell asleep, afterward you know? I found the bag underneath some dirty clothes in the bathroom. Very silently I put on my clothes, took the bag and left. Does that sound bad to you?"

"What?"

"That I stayed with him at night sometimes?"

I had to laugh. "You stole the man's money, but you're worried if I think less of you because you slept with him?"

"I just wondered."

I said, "He couldn't have had the money long if he had it stashed in his bathroom. And you're right: If it was in a paper sack, it isn't honest money. He could've been in the process of delivering it, or it could've been just delivered to him."

I looked at the list again. The candlelight flickered soft and golden on the papers. The vanilla smell was heavy. I said, "I got a feeling we could double this list of names if we knew the history of that money. But the more names we put on the list, the less chance we have of finding the money and the better the chance somebody else already tracked it down. We could be in on the tail end."

Elvia looked glum. She moved both hands in circles on Bug's back. I wasn't saying what she wanted to hear. It wasn't what I wanted to hear either. I said, "Why are you so positive Finney has it?"

"I thought about what you said last time I was here, about who knew besides me and Ricardo? Finney knew I took it, he'd realize Ricardo could have stolen it from me. Ricardo might've talked and it could have gotten back to Finney. He has lots of contacts in our neighborhood."

"Was Ricardo a talker?"

"He was constantly bragging."

"Great. We can probably add half of Pilsen to the list. Why else you sure it's Finney?"

"I can't find him."

"You can't find him because he's scared and hiding, not because he took the money and ran. You say Finney has it, Finney says I have it, I say the Kings have it, the Kings say Finney has it. One big insane circle."

At 11:30 we still sat on the living room floor, talking, when someone banged on the front door hard as a drug cop. Elvia and I looked at each other nervously, then I went to open the door.

It was Finney. In shirt sleeves again, wearing the white shirt he'd worn when Ford picked him up earlier in the day. He swayed in the wind and said, "You've had thirty-six hours instead of twenty-four. Where's my stuff?"

"Why does Elvia call it money and you call it stuff?"

Elvia shouted something from the living room I didn't understand because it was in Spanish. Finney went berserk. He yelled, "That streetwalking slut is here? You two are planning to make a big score at my expense?" He shoved past me, hustled into the living room. Said to Elvia, "You seduce me so you can walk through my house looking for things to steal when I'm asleep? Did he put you up to that? Huh, Miss Messenger Girl? You haven't got brains enough to plan something like that on your own."

She answered in Spanish. Short words, short sentences, contemptuous tone.

He said, "Don't tell me that. I don't believe it, I don't want to hear it." He edged closer to where she sat on the floor. I moved quickly to get in front of him. He pointed his finger at her over my shoulder. Shouted, "*Ramera! Puta! Prostituta!*"

I recognized those words. Then they both were screaming torrents of Spanish, me not understanding a word, but surmising that each was accusing the other of having the money or at least being the reason the other didn't have it. Elvia sprinkled a few English words into her tirade, but for all the good it did me in following what she said she might as well have mixed in Swahili.

Finney moved sideways, left then right, as he shouted, trying to get around me. I moved each time, cutting him off. The people upstairs pounded on the floor. They were a young Mexican couple who barely talked English, which meant they understood every word being said. But they also were straightlaced Catholics and I doubted if understanding Finney and Elvia was as big a treat for them as it would've been for me.

Bugs had retreated into his cage and was cowering, facing away from the room. Three-quarters of the building's occupants wanted quiet. I didn't mind the noise, but I wanted to know what it was all about. I moved behind Finney, wrapped him up in a bear hug, dragged him outside.

Finney continued to shout Spanish into the house and paid no attention to me pulling him. When I got to the bottom step of the porch, wind like a runaway bus whipped around the house corner. It shoved me off balance and Finney and I tumbled to the cold grass. Elvia had followed us to the door. She was still yelling, too.

I got to my feet, looked down at Finney, who'd finally stopped his mouth. I said, "Get the hell out of here or I'll push Elvia out here and it'll be just you and her."

I knew from talking to Santiago that Finney didn't shrink from fighting girls, but I doubted he wanted any part of Elvia Reyes right now.

I was right. He stood up, brushed himself off. Said, "I'm coming back, Kruger. And you and your whore girlfriend better be on guard when I do." Then he walked north to Waveland, bending into the wind, Elvia's screams chasing him.

Only when he was gone around the corner did I remember he owed Joseph Cantel money and I was expected to retrieve it.

THIRTEEN

Back inside, I got Elvia a can of beer, told her to sit on the couch and calm down. She ignored me. Kept pacing down the hallway into the kitchen, then back to the living room, mumbling to herself, not sipping the beer. I could take it for only a minute or two, then I grabbed her hand, pulled her to the couch, shoved her backwards. I sat next to her, shook out two Valiums from the plastic bottle in my pants pocket. Said, "Swallow these."

"What are they?"

"Tranquilizers."

She looked skeptically at the phlegm color pills in my hands, then took both and washed them down. She said, "You got aspirin? I have a headache."

"You have a headache? Look at Bugs." Bugs still fidgeted furiously in the corner of his cage. "He'll be a wreck all night." I brought her two Anacins from the bathroom.

While she swallowed them I said, "I think your theory about Finney just got blown to smithereens."

Her face was wrinkled with worry and excitement. She said, "I think so too. That makes our job harder, doesn't it?"

"At no time did I think it was going to be a day in the park. If you remember, I wasn't convinced he had it to begin with. What were the two of you shouting at each other?"

Suddenly, Elvia began to shake from the aftereffects of the screaming. The can quivered in her hand and beer sloshed out the pop top opening onto her pants. I took the can, set it on the table.

I put my hands around hers, squeezed hard. She smiled weakly. Said, "I don't know all that Orlando was saying. We called each other names. He kept calling me an ignorant Mex farmgirl, a wetback. It's like calling somebody a hillbilly. He said I was a whore and a backstabber. Said you knew where the bag was and I was only here so I could seduce you to get it same as I did with him." She shivered. "I started shouting so hard at the end, I didn't hear what he was saying."

"Wish I understood Spanish. Maybe Finney said something would've helped us."

Elvia said, "Whatever word I think of first, that's what I say. Almost always it's Spanish, but sometimes it's English so I speak in dual tongues. Like 'dumbfuck'. I love to use that word when I'm mad at somebody."

"It gets a certain point across."

"I know. Could you tell the difference in the way we pronounced words? Of course not, what am I asking? You didn't understand one word we said, let alone how we said it. Excuse me, I'm not thinking right now. What I mean is, Finney is half Cuban and Cubans speak more precise and throw their hands around. Puerto Ricans are like that too but not as much. I can tell another Mexican from anybody else Latino. Looks, because we have broader faces, like Indians, but mostly from talk. We like sing when we talk, draw the words out. The people in Mexico City roll their r's like they are drumming. You know, r-r-r-r-r-r." It did indeed sound like someone rolling sticks on a snare drum. "But now I can understand anybody who speaks Spanish.

Except Mexicans from Texas. Chicanos? They talk terrible. They mix English and Spanish until it's so blended only they can understand each other."

"Tex-Mex?"

"Yep. The words they use aren't even words. They fuck up both languages."

She laid back and rested her head. After some seconds she said, "I talk pretty good English now, don't I?"

"Good as me."

She smiled. "I took lots of courses downtown and I never speak Spanish unless I have to. Lots of Mexicans have been here fifteen years or more and they can barely speak English because they don't need to. What with the neighborhoods and the newspapers and the TV stations and everything that's in Spanish. Sometimes I speak Spanish because there's Latin people who are insulted if you speak English to them and they don't speak it so well. Like you think you are superior or showing off. Sometimes when I'm downtown speaking Spanish with someone, Americans stare at me like I'm breaking a law. One time an old lady said to me, 'Speak English, you're in America now.' Like we were talking about her. What would those people do if they were in Mexico City or Havana and they met another Chicago person and neither of them spoke Spanish very well? Speak English, right?"

"Sure, but Americans don't think past red, white, and blue and Chicagoans aren't world famous for racial tolerance anyway."

"It's just more comfortable, more free, you know, to speak Spanish to another Latin."

I said, "I wasn't offended by you and Finney. Just curious about what you said."

Elvia grinned self-consciously. "I know," she said, "I'm just talking. The shouting and the wind got me excited, and when I get worked up I talk nonstop. You can ignore me."

"Okay."

She said, "The pills are helping." She yawned.

"They always do."

"Kruger, you really don't know where the bag is, do you?"

"No. Finney's just scared. He doesn't know what he's talking about. I still think a King has it, but I'm not positive. Maybe it's someone we never heard of. What did Finney mean when he said 'Did he put you up to this?'"

She shrugged. "Ricardo, I guess."

"Anybody else?"

Elvia shook her head. "I don't know." She stared at the candles on the floor "It's not going to be as easy as I thought."

I went to the kitchen, removed my stash from under the sink. Stood at the table and rolled a fat joint, went back and handed it to Elvia. Lit her up. We passed it back and forth until it was finished, then began sipping at our beers to wash away the smoke. I lit a Kool, put my feet up on the coffee table. The wind was still shuddering the house, but neither of us jumped from it now.

I said, "You been here seven years?"

"Uh huh."

"Illegally?"

She nodded.

"You worry about getting caught?"

"Not very much anymore."

"How'd you get up here?"

"Crossed the river like everybody else. First two times I didn't make it."

"What happened?"

"When I got caught? Nothing. They stick you in kind of like a jail a little while. When they get enough wetbacks, they cram them all in a school bus, drive it a hundred miles into Mexico and open the door. Everybody out. I signed a form both times, promised I wouldn't try again. Third time I made it."

"You cross in the water or over a bridge?"

"Water."

"Water's safer?"

"Easier. Unless you drown, which some people do. There's twelve bridges cross the Rio Grande, but not many illegals use them because they got turnstiles and they're lit up at night. Border men look at cards and stuff. Fake cards cost more down there than here. I crossed below the International Bridge at Nuevo Laredo. Most women and families cross at Juarez-El Paso because the Grande is only a stream there and you can wade it.

They joke that to be a wetback crossing at Juarez you have to take a bath first. But Juarez was too far away."

"You had to swim?"

"Nope. Only part of me got wet was the tips of my toes. I put my one extra dress and some tortillas and two six-packs of Pepsi Cola in one of those plastic garbage bags and hired a boy to carry me over on his shoulders. The boys call themselves mules."

"What's a mule cost?"

"About a dime. They do it all night, back and forth, carrying women and children. I was in a group of ten or eleven people from my town. We all crossed and then started walking for San Antonio. We walked through the countryside using these tall red tower lights as our guide. All the towns have them. Of course, we couldn't walk on the highway or through the towns. We walked way around Laredo because we heard it was so easy to get picked up there. It was neon-lit, looked very dangerous. Outside there, all the way to San Antonio in fact, the land is flat and dry like chalk dust with brush bigger than me. Not desert but close. A man in our group had been back and forth a lot of times so he led us. He made the trip so many times he recognized the towns by the lights high in the air. I think he said they were for radio stations. We slept or sat around during the day and walked after dark, which is why we had to use the red lights. To be sure we were going in the right direction. The only town name I remember is Dilley. On the third night, we got to Pearsall. On the outskirts in an auto garage, we met a real thin Chicano who looked like a hired killer. He gave us a ride to San Antonio. I knew for sure I'd make it then."

"Why for sure?"

"I don't know, I just knew. Before that, we were scared because the man who led us kept saying to be on the lookout for the redneck gangs. He said they hid in the brush and shot down *mojados* for sport. He told us the rednecks are never arrested or reprimanded. It's like they're shooting quail or gophers. And the Border Patrol considers them like allies because they can't catch all the wets and they believe these gangs take care of some of the overflow. I'm not so sure I believe that now, but I did then."

"Sounds like redneck behavior to me."

"It might be true. My brother said he was shot at when he crossed, but my brother all the time lied to make himself a hero."

"How'd you get to Chicago?"

Elvia yawned, grinned, then sat for some stoned seconds, remembering. "I must of been a hilarious sight. Sixteen years old. I weighed maybe eighty pounds. Thick black hair to my waist. I put it up in a bun all the time. Only English I could say was 'Fuck you' and 'Chicago, Illinois' and I didn't know what the first one meant. I thought it meant 'thank you.' I had an envelope with my aunt's address written on it in my second dress. Blue Island Avenue, Chicago, Illinois. In San Antonio, they have these vans called *las trocas*, which are like a wetback taxi service. Run straight from there to Chicago. They go from Laredo to San Antonio, too, but we didn't know that. It wasn't expensive, but it took almost all my money. I rode here packed in the back of a van. No windows of course because somebody might see in. Two girls and twenty-two men. We all smelled very bad to start with, we hadn't bathed for days. And you know the kind of sweat people make when they're scared? There were two drivers, Mexicans, and they ignored us the whole drive. They stopped only three times all the way here. One drove while the other slept. If you had to go to the bathroom, you held it. The men would turn their backs and pee into tin coffee cans and they'd all giggle and the other girl and me would stare away, pretending not to hear. We sat together, Lupe and me, holding on to each other like we would collapse if we let go. Lupe died last year walking to the grocery store when two gangs started shooting at each other."

"She a close friend?"

"After the ride, yes."

"What time of year'd you come up?"

"December." She made a short laugh. "Figures, huh? The more north we came, the colder we got and we didn't have warm clothes. We complained to the drivers we were cold, but they ignored us."

"What else did you talk about?"

"The men talked. Lupe and I never said one word the whole

trip, except whispers to each other. Like 'Are you okay?' and stuff. They talked about money and *La Migra*, the two things every illegal talks about. They discussed the large amounts of money they would make in Chicago and how they planned to spend it. And they discussed ways to outfox *La Migra*. They're the enemy you know. You have the Russians, we have *La Migra*."

I said, "Lots of people get angry about illegal aliens. When the economy gets depressed like it is now for blue collar workers, they get real angry."

She still had some fire left. She bent forward, banged the beer can hard on the table, turned to face me. Said, "My forefathers were Indians. They migrated north to south, from here to Mexico, so if you want to be technical about all this, I am the native, you are the alien. I'm just coming home. Anglos act like we are foreigners. The Southwest is an extension of Mexico. We used to own that land until you took it away. England is foreign, France is foreign, Germany is foreign. So you whites are descendents of foreigners, I'm not. My people have always been on this continent. A boundary is just a line marked in dirt anyway."

I assumed I was hearing the standard IA justification argument. If any was needed. I had to admit it wasn't bad. I said, "I never called you foreign, but you are illegal so you have to be careful. You shouldn't be getting involved in screaming matches in residential neighborhoods at midnight. You get arrested, you go home."

She leaned back, said, "You're right," and was quiet. A minute later she snored softly. Twenty milligrams of Valium does that to people who aren't used to it.

I lowered her torso to the couch, raised her legs up and laid them on the armrest, slid off her scuffed blue jogging shoes. I brought a blanket and pillow from the bedroom, slipped the pillow under head and floated the blanket over her. I made sure Bugs was asleep and blew out the candles.

FOURTEEN

I set the alarm for seven. Elvia was still asleep on the couch when it rang me awake. I left a note that said I'd be back before noon and we'd start searching for "her" money then.

The windstorm had stopped, the morning was golden and gorgeous. The kind of fresh spring day that after five months of frigid air, dirty snow, and bare trees makes you want to chuck everything and hit the road with your thumb out. Makes you feel like today really *is* the first day of the rest of your life.

People in the Loop felt it, too. A few actually smiled hello and nobody growled at me to look the hell where I was going when I got trapped between groups of business-suited men and women striding to work.

I waited an hour, leaning against the front door of the Midnight Lounge, for Cantel. A young woman walking by said, "You need it *that* bad, buddy?" and laughed. I thought of a witty retort when she was a block away.

Cantel arrived at 9:30, lumbering across Wabash like a fullback crashing off tackle. He was fifteen feet away when he saw me. He smiled crookedly. Said, "Cubbies won yesterday. Worst they can do is one and one-sixty-one."

"I can always hope for that."

He said, "You here to tell me you found Finney already?"

"Seen him twice since you hired me. One time with Stacey Ford, one time without."

Cantel stopped walking for a second and his face changed into equal parts confusion and anger. Then he resumed walking and unlocked the door. I followed him inside.

He flipped on a bank of blue lights over the bar. We moved under the bluish fog, climbed on adjoining stools. He said, very quiet, "So where is Finney now?"

"Now? I don't know. But Ford can tell you easy enough. When did Ford come to you with his proposition about me finding Finney? Yesterday?"

"It was a coincidence like I told you. Ford worked for me the last couple months. I knew he was a friend of Finney's, but that's all."

"Save it. I can check things like that, you know? You telling me you two just happened to be sitting around shooting the shit over a beer and you asked into all this by coincidence looks pretty pathetic from where I'm sitting. When'd he approach you?"

Cantel lit a cigarette, blew out smoke. Said, "Okay. He stopped by night before last. We've known each other about a year, not real good, but as acquaintances. He knew Finney owed me money because he's been working for Finney, something to do with the shadow labor market, whatever that is. He said he suspected Finney was looking to stiff him and everybody else he owes money to. I perked my ears, got a little pissed. He told me Finney had been ripped off of a bundle of money, but was getting it back. Said Finney thought the money ended up in your hands somehow. Ford was pretty sure you didn't have it. He said Finney had dropped out of sight and Ford thought using you we could locate him. Said you're pretty decent at scaring up people. He asked if I'd front you the fee to find him for us and then we'd both get our money."

"Ford told you he'd lost track of Finney?"

Cantel didn't answer. He twisted the bar stool with his butt, galloped his fingers on the bar. He breathed deep like he was suppressing a great anger.

I said, "You didn't want what Finney owes you, if he even owes you anything. When Ford told you the story about the bag of money, you decided you wanted it. Just like everybody else involved in this mess, including me. Ford offer fifty-fifty?"

No answer.

I said, "How much does Finney owe you?"

"A grand about."

"And that's the only reason Ford came to you? Because Finney owes you money which would make you interested in finding him if he was blowing town?"

"I guess."

"Guess again. What does Ford care if you ever got your money from Finney? And why'd Ford come to you and why'd you two hire me to find Finney if Ford knew where Finney was all the time?"

"I'd like to know the answer to that more than you."

"Ford played you for a moron, Cantel. You understand my consternation here, don't you? I'm not calling you a liar, but you understand the whole story is hard for me to follow?"

"Yeah. How'd you find out Ford was lying?"

"Followed him."

"To where?"

I gave him the Parkside address. Said, "But Finney won't be there anymore, which is why I'm not demanding the hundred twenty five you'd owe me if he was."

"You sure he's not there now?"

"Pretty sure. I don't think he's gonna stay in any one place very long. The man is scared and something happened yesterday to make him even more scared. He almost got snuffed by some hostile gangbangers while he was with Ford."

"Did Ford set him up?"

"I hadn't thought of that, but it's possible."

"Who else wants Finney?"

I said, "Lots of people want that bag."

Cantel threw his cigarette to the floor, clapped his hands together like he was mashing a mosquito. "When I get my hands on Ford."

"I don't think you'll be seeing Ford again. How much did he take you for?"

"I loaned him three hundred bucks."

I smiled. "You gave him three hundred bucks."

Cantel said, "So what was the story? Him coming to me like that?"

"Someone wanted us to meet each other. I have to find out who and why. You'd automatically assume Finney, but I don't have any idea what the hell Ford is up to. You mixed up in any illegal enterprises, Cantel?"

"I own this nightclub, a couple liquor stores. Unsavory maybe, not illegal."

"Drugs?"

"I told you, me and jail wouldn't mix."

"This is just a wild stab because of Finney, but you involved with illegal aliens?

"I probably hired some."

"Not now?"

"I check for green cards, but I don't check a card to make sure it's authentic.

"That's the shadow labor market Ford referred to."

"See, I don't even know the term."

"You speak Spanish?"

"Just swear words."

"If that's true, you are the first person I met—Anglo or Latin—on this case who doesn't. Lately, I feel like a tourist in my own town."

FIFTEEN

I drove back to the apartment. I was glad I'd seen Cantel face to face. He'd joined the ever expanding club of worried "bag" people the second I explained the situation to him. He was worried because he couldn't understand why Ford was jacking him around. I could tell from his eyes. He could've bluffed me over the phone, but not in person. I needed to find out who wanted him dumped into this mess. Obviously he wanted to find that out, too. I also needed to know why, but I suspected Cantel already knew the answer to that.

Elvia and Bugs were on the couch, watching a game show on TV. She was drinking coffee and eating powdered doughnuts out of a long box open on the coffee table in front of her. She'd fed little doughnut pieces to Bugs; powder sugar caked his pink nose.

I said, "Don't you be giving my rabbit diabetes."

"Where'd you go?"

"Out."

"Out where?"

"See a friend."

"If we are partners, you should tell me everthing you are doing. Not leave little notes for when I wake up and nobody's here."

"Bugs was here."

"I'm serious. I should of gone."

"It didn't involve you."

"I should be involved in everything."

"You're gonna be. We're going to see some Romeo Kings."

Her face changed from annoyance to fear. "When?"

"Now."

"Why?"

"You want your money? We've so far ruled out Orlando Finney and we've ruled out you and me. Now we check out Romeo Kings. We haven't got many leads so we work on the ones we got. Luis Santiago told me two days ago he'd set up a meeting for me with the Kings. You know Luis?"

"I've heard of him." She paused. "I don't think I'm going to see the Kings."

"They won't hurt you if you're with me. They want me healthy in case I should lead them to Finney. He's after me, they're after him. Means I'm useful to them."

"You don't realize the kind of people they are."

"Sure I do. Gangbangers. Treat them the way a snake handler treats rattlesnakes. Lots of respect, be ready to run like hell if they get pissed."

Santiago wasn't in when I called, so half an hour later, Elvia and I drove up Lincoln Avenue. I went very slow up and down for two blocks on either side of the office building, but I didn't see the silver Dodge or any other car crammed with Romeo Kings. I said, "Either they already got Finney, or they figure he's smart enough not to come back here after yesterday. I'll assume the latter." I parked, we went inside.

Enrique Medina sat behind my desk. The muscle boy with the Rand McNally face sat on the corner of it, tapping a pen on his thigh. The Rabbit hadn't made this trip. The two wore baggy faded jeans and green sweatshirts. Marvin sat behind his own desk looking painfully "normal," leafing through some insurance pamphlet he held upside down.

Medina said something in Spanish to Elvia. She stared at the floor, muttered some words. Medina smiled wide, said some more Spanish. Elvia said, "Elvia Reyes," in lilting, musical Spanish; it sounded nothing like when I pronounced it. Medina stopped smiling. He said to me, "Your partner, eh? You two are not looking for Orlando Finney by any chance?"

"Actually, we were looking for you. We want the money and he hasn't got it. We know that."

"You don't have to look for Orlando Finney because you know where he is, right? You could probably tell me where he is this very second."

"How you figure that?"

"Yesterday, we waited here all day." He pointed north. "Right down the street there. You never showed, but he did. We chased him and some blonde Anglo guy halfway down Lincoln, but we lost them when a light turned red on us." He smiled a self satisfied smile. "That's how I figure that. That's also how I figure he keeps in contact with you."

"Not with me. He might've dropped by to see if I have the bag. He keeps doing that in case I turn up with it."

Medina said, "I think you're a liar."

I said, "That concerns me, what you think. I think a Romeo King has that bag of money. I think the King who went up to Ricardo Reyes' room an hour before I did has it. You wouldn't of been that King would you?"

Medina barked a laugh. "I look like I just came into some money, don't I? It was the clothes gave it away I bet. You think I'd be here now if I had a big bag of American dollars?"

"You admit the bag is what you want, not Finney?"

"I don't admit nothin' to you."

"Last time, you insisted all you wanted was Orlando Finney. You never heard of the stolen money."

"That still goes. I want Finney."

"Why?"

"What do you care? I want him, that's all you need to know."

"Any Kings taken off the last couple of days? Dropped out of sight? Returned to Mexico?"

"You're the one person I'd tell if they had."

Elvia and Rand McNally had been intently following the conversation, moving their eyes from speaker to speaker, Medina's buddy keeping a smartass sneer on his mouth. For the hell of it I said, "If you guys have the money, we'll go fifty-fifty and Finney'll never hear about it."

Elvia exploded in a burst of Spanish. Medina stared at her for a long second, then growled, "*Collarse.*" Elvia shut up, but she glared at Medina. He stared at her, then at me. Said, "I'm going to be back and I'm going to keep my eyes on both of you." They left the office, walking in exaggerated macho-slowness.

The second the door closed behind them, Marvin was on his feet. He shouted, "That's it! You are out of here, Daniel. You think a hundred twenty five bucks a month compensates me for being humiliated in my own office by dirt like that? You're gone, you're history!" He started to pace back and forth in front of his desk. Elvia and I watched as he turned, strode, turned, strode. He was as scared as anybody I'd ever seen, including me on many occasions.

I said, "What'd they do to you?"

He threw his arms outward, waved them around like egg beaters. "They walk in here like they own the place. Sauntering, picking things up and looking them over, shoving my papers off the desk. This is my building, Daniel, remember? *My* building. You came to me and asked for office space. I sure didn't ask you. I got along fine for years without your measly one hundred and twenty five dollars. I've put up with a parade of these subhumans you call clients, but this is it. Those walking sacks of slime—" He sliced the air horizontally with both hands, continued pacing. "They sit here, they grin insolently at me because they know I can't do anything to them. They say things like 'scaredygringo' just loud enough so I can hear and then they giggle. And if I were to say anything, they'd probably beat me up or throw me outside naked or something."

I said, "I don't know about the naked bit. I don't think they're that tough."

Marvin stopped, stared at me, muttered, "Yeah, it's real funny, isn't it?" Then he marched out the front door.

Elvia said, "Will he really kick you out?"

"He might. He's just an insurance salesman. He doesn't deal much with street punks. Freaked him out, didn't it?"

She said, "What do we do now?"

"Talk to Stacey Ford again."

"Why Ford?"

"Ford's got all ten fingers in this. Finney, Cantel, us—we've only got a couple each. I want to learn some things about Joseph Cantel. I want to find out who Fords works for besides himself."

"I hate Stacey Ford."

"That's not what he implies."

"Figures he'd talk about that. I want you to know it wasn't my idea. I don't want to see him. Besides, he knows I set you after him to find Ricardo."

"I squared all that. You can't duck every meeting I set up. You complained this morning when I went off without you, now you complain every time I wanna take you with me. You want the money or not?"

"Of course I do."

"It's not gonna come looking for you."

Elvia stiffened; I was calling her a coward. She said, "No shit."

"What did Medina ask you when we walked in?"

"Nothing."

"Tell me. I know it was nothing good."

"He asked if you were paying me enough for sex."

"What'd you answer?"

"That he had it wrong. You and I were just working together."

"And then he asked your name?"

"Yes."

"And when he heard Elvia Reyes, he knew what we were working on. What did you say at the end, before he told you to shut up?"

"After you said fifty-fifty, I told him you didn't speak for me. I told him I wasn't splitting my money with a gang of junkies, especially junkies who killed my brother."

"But you didn't care about your brother, so why get so outraged?"

"That's beside the point."

I said, "No, it isn't. It wasn't your brother got you so mad, it was thinking of losing some of the money. You are one greedy girl."

"And you plan to give yours away to the Salvation Army?"

Bingo. I said, "Let's find Stacey Ford."

SIXTEEN

It was three o'clock, still sunny, when Ford stumbled out of The Dangerous Game. We were parked behind his yellow Chevy half a block south of the bar.

I yelled his name out the window while he tried to fit his key in the drivers door lock. He stared at me for a few seconds, weaving slightly as if he were standing on a water bed. Then he lurched to my window, looked inside. Said, "Beautiful day, ain't it?"

I agreed.

"Followin' me?"

"Nobody has to follow you, Ford. They just sit outside this bar and wait for you to leave."

He glared at the bar like it had betrayed him; then looked back inside the car. He said, "Elvia, how've you been?"

She didn't answer. Ford giggled, then sneezed. He kept staring past me at her. "You mad at me, Elvia?" he asked.

She didn't answer again.

"Imagine that," he said. "And Ricardo said you were sweet on me." He pressed his nostrils together with thumb and forefinger.

I said, "Tell me about Joseph Cantel."

"What about him?"

"Why'd you two give me that song and dance about hunting for Finney?"

"That was no song and dance, Dan. Every word was legit."

"I talked to Cantel this morning. He says he barely knew you before you showed up night before last."

He smiled, flipped his bangs back with his hand. "Caught, eh? So what?" He nodded at Elvia. "Why you two together?"

I said, "We're looking for Elvia's money."

"Elvia's money, is it?"

Elvia had stared at the rear of Ford's car the entire conversation. Now she swung her head our way, stared at Ford. She said, "Yes, my money."

Ford gave Elvia's body a caressing visual frisk, remembering probably. She was a looker in the tight jeans and sweater. He said, "You ain't gonna find it sittin' in cars with this guy."

She said, "Why not?"

"Because I got it." He smiled like the Cheshire cat, then started sneezing again. He pinched his nostrils and the sneezes stopped.

Elvia and I looked at each other. My mind raced, figuring. I turned to Ford and said, "You tell the truth about as often as the Pentagon."

"I got it," he said, defensively. "Got it this morning matter of fact. You have to realize I knew a little more about all this than you did. That's why I'm at the bar. I'm celebrating. I'm leaving tonight."

"Leaving for where?"

"South."

"That includes a lot of territory."

"I ain't so drunk I'm gonna tell you exactly where I'm goin'."

Elvia turned in the seat so she faced us. She looked from Ford to me, back to Ford, her eyes curious. She said, "How'd you get it?"

"What's that matter?"

I said, "Elvia, this guy is bombed. He's got coke sitting on top of booze, he's horny as hell. He'd claim he just saw Elvis in that bar if he thought it would get your clothes off."

She whispered, "But what if he *has* got it?"

"He doesn't."

Ford reached into his jean jacket pocket, pulled out some currency, made a fan out of six twenty dollar bills and waved them in front of my face. Said, "Here's part of it."

"That's exactly one hundred twenty dollars, Ford. Even I carry that much money sometimes."

He pulled a folded in half thick roll of bills from his pants pocket, shoved it in front of me, quickly removed it.

Elvia said, "That's my money, Stacey. I want it."

Ford cackled. Said, "You ain't in no position to be ordering orders, chiquita. But tell you what. You come along with me now, we'll work something out. I ain't such a hard guy to get along with, but I can be a hard guy, remember?" He winked, licked his lips.

Elvia looked at me, brows raised over confused eyes. She kept sneaking glances at Ford, who continued to wave the six twenties in front of me.

I muttered, "He hasn't got it, Elvia. If he did, why would he offer any to you?"

She whispered, "But the money? That was a huge roll."

"Cantel loaned him money yesterday. That's probably what's left of it. That roll could be all singles. It'd only be another hundred or so if it is."

Ford leered at Elvia. He said something in slow, halting Spanish. Elvia answered him rapid fire. Right then I knew I was out of it. They continued to talk Spanish. As they did, I repeated, "He doesn't have it, Elvia."

He stopped talking. Said, "Well?" and waited some seconds. Then he said, "Okay Elvia, last chance. I got the money. You comin' with or you wanna sit here torturing yourself and end up wondering about it all night?" He walked back to his car.

Elvia scrambled out of the Skylark. Before she closed the door, she leaned in and said, "I've got to find out." Then she slammed the door and ran to the Chevy.

SEVENTEEN

After they drove off, I sat there for a few minutes, shaking my head. Then I drove to the Guild Bookstore on Lincoln and purchased a Spanish-English Dictionary. In the Skylark I leafed through it. 226 easy-to-read pages it said on the orange and yellow cover. B's were v's, y's were j's, no h's, you got to tatoo your tongue against the roof of your mouth to say r. If you were the guy whose name was under the title, maybe it was easy to read. Frankly, I was having a little trouble.

I drove to the Loop, parked below Pago-Pago, went to the Midnight Lounge. Suppertime, only a few businessmen were scattered in the dim, red-tinged darkness drinking and watching a silicone-enhanced blonde in a tiny black bikini prance back and forth on the bandstand. To her right sat a solitary black saxophonist who blew a pattern of discordant notes over and over.

I asked the two bartenders if Cantel was in. Both said no. I said it was important. The second one, a thin middle-aged man with an eye tic, said, "His girlfriend lives on Ohio Street." He gave me the address. Said, "He might be there. Usually is around this time. You learned it from someone else."

So I crept through rush hour traffic to Ohio Street. Cantel's girlfriend opened the door clutching a highball glass. She was a hard-faced brunette, fortyish. She stared at me with no interest.

I said, "I'm a friend of Joseph's. He here?"

"The name?"

"Dan Kruger."

She brushed wisps of hair up off her forehead, her eyes perked a little. She said, "He left. Dan Kruger, you say? Funny, Joseph mentioned your name today a number of times, but I never got the impression he considers you a friend."

"Where is he?"

"He didn't say where he left for. If he had he wouldn't want me telling you."

"You got any ideas?"

"Ordinarily I might, but when he left he was in a state I've never seen before. Like things were on his mind he wished weren't there."

"What did he say about me?"

"To be honest, if somebody were to have asked me what your name was before you just introduced yourself, I would of said Goddamn-Dan-Kruger. Everytime he said your name that's how it came out. He said you could maybe ruin his life. He frequently gets over dramatic, but I think he was serious this time. When I asked him what was the matter, he shut up. Usually he tells me everything. Well, almost everything. Nobody tells somebody everything. It was scary watching him. I've never seen him like that. Maybe you should tell me what's going on."

"I can't. I don't know. Somebody wanted I should meet him. I'm involved with people who smuggle wetbacks and somebody who kills 'em. Joseph tells me he isn't mixed up in either smuggling or murder. So what's he worried about?"

"It's none of your business what he's involved in, so I'd be inclined to tell you to go screw yourself if I did know."

"Well, there's our problem. I don't know, you don't know, only Joseph knows."

Back at the Midnight Lounge nobody had moved. Under the weak stage light the girl still strutted, the saxophonist still blew. The suits still sipped and stared, waiting for the fun to start. Because the skinny bartender was such a pal of mine, I asked him where Cantel's office was.

He said, "Ain't back yet." He licked his lips, blinked his eyes rapidly.

"All the better."

"You ain't a regular."

I wasn't sure what he meant so I shrugged.

"What business you got in his office?"

"Wanna wait for him."

"Uh huh. You don't wanna snoop?"

"Just wait."

"You could wait for him here and drink while you're doing it."

"Too noisy."

He looked around the almost deserted room, grinned. "It *is* loud in here, ain't it? His office is a popular hangout. How bad you wanna wait there?"

I removed my wallet, put a five on the bar.

He smiled sadly, shook his head. "You wanna see him about as bad as one of these briefcase boys wants to see his wife stroll through the front door over there."

I put another five on top of the first one. He shook his head again. I winced, added a ten.

He slid the money toward him, stuffed it in his apron, then said, "Follow," and we walked the length of the bar—me on the outside, him inside. We turned left at the end of it, pushed through a heavy wood door that opened to a concrete floored hallway illuminated by a single naked light bulb. We walked about thirty yards, went down a flight of five stairs. At the bottom on our left, the bartender pushed open a second door, said, "Cantel's office. You found it on your own." He left.

I flicked on an overhead light. The office was tiny, containing only a dented metal desk and swivel chair and a long green couch. On brown walls were large fight posters, curling concavely like giant yellow blisters. All were dated late Sixties. I read them over.

Cantel had fought as a heavyweight, and been a professional "opponent." His name was at the bottom of each poster. I'd never heard of any of the guys he'd fought, which didn't surprise me. Of course, Chicago hasn't produced a decent fighter in years and boxing bores me anyway since Ali quit. I hadn't heard of most of the headliners either. He fought as 'Ironjaw' Joseph Cantelli. Cantelli meant he'd wanted the city's sizable Italian population for his fandom. 'Ironjaw' probably meant he was the kind of stiff who regularly got beaten bloody and senseless, but wouldn't hit the canvas if his opponent nailed him from behind with a tire iron.

The desk was covered with folded newspapers, old *Hustler* magazines, and racing forms. A pile of memos was on one side. I leafed through them. Business notes mostly—a reminder that Cindy had a raise coming, a note from a Lamar Jackson that the Midnight Lounge was a month delinquent on a bill. Didn't say what for. Another note said to have CD stop by for "fun." There were more but they told me nothing.

I went through the desk drawers. Mounds of paper that meant nothing to me; a couple of Polaroid snaps of nude girls sitting on the green couch looking bored. Probably hoping to work at the club; they sure weren't trying out for *Playboy*.

Next to the telephone was a small piece of paper ripped from a phone book. I recognized it as phone book paper right away. It's thin and pulpy and I use it to roll pot when I'm out of One Point Five's and I'm too stoned to go out for more. There were four phone numbers written in red ink on the paper. The pen was still lying next to the phone. "Ed" was written next to the first number. "Alton" next to the second. "C" by the third. The fourth number had no name by it. Below the numbers was a lot of doodling—faces, stars, the word ALL traced a lot of times, next to it a dollar sign. And the word DREAMER underlined over and over. Cantel had been on the phone for a while.

I wrote the names and phone numbers in my notebook, took one last look around, then left. I nodded to the bartender as I walked past, but he pretended not to see me.

EIGHTEEN

At the office, Marvin was still gone but a note was on my desk. It said, *We gotta talk—M.T.* I whispered, "Anytime, Marvin", crumpled the note and tossed it in the wastebasket. I sat down, dialed the first number and asked for Ed.

An exasperated male voice said, "Who wants him?"

"I'm calling for Joseph Cantel."

"For Godsakes, Cantel just called."

"Yeah? He told me to call you."

"When'd he say this?"

"This morning."

"About what?"

I said, "The usual."

He was silent for a bit, then said in a confused voice, "I think you're assuming I'm a little denser than your average dink. If Cantel's around, put him on."

"That's why I'm calling. He ain't here."

"Where is he?"

"Out of town."

The voice was silent for some more seconds. He said, "Bullshit. He was in town less than an hour ago. Like I said, he called then so whatever it was he wanted you to talk to Ed about he took care of it himself."

I said, "I'm supposed to ask Ed how many workers he needs tomorrow."

Just a guess. And a bad one. The voice barked a laugh. Said, "Workers? What the fuck're you talking about? I bet you wouldn't know Joseph Cantel from Joseph Blowjob."

"How would I get this number if I didn't know Cantel? How would I know to ask for Ed? I don't understand the suspicion here."

"I bet you don't even know Ed."

"Sure I know Ed. I told you I work for Cantel."

The voice said, "This is Ed and Ed don't know you. So fuck off." The phone slammed in my ear.

I dialed the second number. Said, "This is Joseph Cantel. Alton there?"

After a second spent assimilating my voice, a deep voice said, "Hell you are, buddy" and hung up.

I was tearing it up. Where the hell was Rich Little when you needed him?

I dialed the third number. Said I was an associate of Joseph Cantel needing to talk to "C." A black male voice with a pronounced drawl said, "Cantel? He still comin', ain't he?"

"Sure."

"Hour ago he says he'll be here thirty minutes. I got people hurtin' here."

"He just now called. Forgot your address."

"Come on, man. Nobody enjoys dealin' with amateurs. When I was down to his office, he was talking like he's some kinda Caucasian Superfly. This makes him look like a teenager pushin' reefer."

I put some irritation in my voice. "Hey, man. He's got a lot of people to take care of."

"But he was here one time for Chrissakes. The man tastin' his own product? People shouldn't forget nothin' when talking this kind of cash, man. You understand what I'm sayin'? I'm on Roosevelt Road, across from Gerald's Sandwich Shop. Three story brick. Only brick on the block."

"He's callin' right back. I'll tell him."

"When's he gonna show?"

"Before you know it. How much you want?"

"Same as the first time. I got to retalk the entire conversation I had with him with you?"

"Relax. Same price?"

"Same like before. Twenty-five hundred for seventy five. Jesus."

"Hang tight, my man."

The fourth number was answered by a giggly female voice that sounded like the owner was floating near the ceiling. But the girl wasn't so trashed, she thought I maybe worked for Joseph Cantel.

NINETEEN

Forty-five minutes later, I was parked across the street from a brick three-flat on Roosevelt Road. Gerald's Bar-B-Que Sandwich Shop was a tiny, unpainted wooden building that looked ready to cave in, with just a teeny purple neon sign in the window, but the smell drifting from it was divine and many people went in and out the front door. I lit a Kool, fought the urge to run inside for a sandwich. I was sure Cantel would show and I didn't want to miss him standing in line at a cash register.

At 8:30, he entered the brick building, after pausing at the top of the front steps to look left and right. My plan was to give him time to get into "C's" apartment, then knock on doors until

I found him. I wasn't going to get fancy. Just ask what the hell was going on. If I was lucky maybe he'd actually tell me.

I gave him three minutes. Just as I was opening the car door, I heard something that could have been a gunshot coming from inside the three-flat. It wasn't loud—no pedestrian seemed to hear it—and because nobody on the street stopped or pointed, I started to wonder if I'd heard anything.

All three levels of the building had large bay windows in front. The one on the top floor was partially open. Seconds after the shot, the lamp behind the window on the top floor blinked out. Somewhere inside that apartment, a red lamp was on, making a faded light in the front room, then it went out too. A minute later, Cantel pushed open the front door and hurried west, hands in his jacket pockets, staring at the sidewalk in front of his steps.

I hated to lose Cantel, but I had to know what happened on the top floor of the three-flat, so I waited two minutes. Figured then that he wasn't coming back. Waited some more. The lights did not come back on, no one screamed "Murder!" out the window, nobody ran from the building panic stricken.

I let myself in, walked gingerly up the dark stairwell. The top floor door was ajar; Cantel had left in a big hurry. I pushed it open. On the interior side of the door, there was three chainlink locks and a gold double-bolt lock above the door knob. Nobody could've forced their way into this place.

I pushed the door shut behind me with my butt, flipped on the overhead light. I was in the kitchen. Empty cans of spaghettio's and pork and beans were open and smelling rank on the counter and table. Dishes with brown crust were stacked high in a dry, deep sink. The garbage can overflowed, more cans and paper plates had slid over the top of it onto the floor.

In the next room, drug paraphenalia was scattered on a wooden coffee table—sandwich bags, spoons with bent-down handles, pop bottle caps burned black, books of matches. Sifted into the ruts of cigarette burn marks were granules of powder like brown sugar. At one end of the room, fifty or so phonograph records had been rolled from their covers onto the floor. One red and white hightop Air Jordan basketball shoe was on a black beanbag chair in that corner. The table, the beanbag chair, and a

26-inch TV console was the only furniture in the room.

The body was in the bedroom, the room after the living room. A black male. On the floor at the foot of the bed. He wore gray slacks and a black on black striped polyester shirt. There was a wet hole in the middle of the shirt above where his heart used to beat. The sleeve of one arm was rolled up over his skinny bicep and a needle with syringe attached emerged from the inner crook of his elbow below a twisted tight strip of rubber. The dead man's head was turned away from the door, facing under the bed. I stood over him, put my index finger on his nose and moved his head to the right far enough to see his face. His eyes were open, he seemed to smile slightly. He looked twenty-five or so.

I went through the dresser drawers, looked under the bed, moved around the closet, then went back to the living room. Found mail on the TV set with the building's address. Two names, Curtis Hopkins and May Carter. I went back to the bedroom, removed the dead man's wallet, shifting him carefully to avoid the pool of blood that was getting larger on his left side. The only ID I could find was an expired State Identification Card issued in 1980. The name on it was Clayton Hopkins, and even though the picture was five years old, I could tell it wasn't a picture of the dead man. I put the wallet back. Could think of nothing else to look for.

I went back to the Skylark, leaving the apartment door not quite closed, just like I'd found it.

At nine o'clock a tall black man and an emaciated white woman went inside the building. The third floor lit up. After only five minutes, the couple came back out walking fast and laughing and looking over their shoulders. They'd known where Hopkins kept his stash. They were so delighted at finding free junk they could easily overlook a dead man in the bedroom, even if the dead man was their connection. Junkies can always find a connection; they don't often find free dope.

Ten minutes after that, a thin-as-bones black woman, wearing jeans and a long black coat, started up the steps. I yelled, "Yo, May, across the street."

The woman turned and squinted my way. I yelled, "You May Carter?" She continued to stare, then jaywalked Roosevelt, stopping ten feet from the car. She said, "Who are you?" She leaned over and looked inside, searching my face in the dim light from the streetlamps and moving cars. Her face was drawn and pockmarked. She said, "I ain't recognizing you. What you want?"

"I just saw Curtis."

"So what?"

"Get in the car a minute. I have to tell you something. You're gonna get hit you stay there." Cars were having to swerve to avoid her, some honked.

She moved a step closer. Said, "Tell me here. I hear you fine. I don't get in cars with strange men. My momma taught me that much."

"You live with Curtis Hopkins?"

"Maybe."

"Why does he use Clayton Hopkin's ID? That his brother?"

"Was his brother. He's dead."

"Curtis can't get ID?"

"Maybe he rather use somebody else's. How you know what ID he carries anyway?"

"You like Curtis?"

"Do I *like* him?"

"Yeah."

"Maybe I do, maybe I don't. Why?"

"The something I have to tell you is about him. If you genuinely like the man, I might word it different."

Her expression changed slightly. She suspected what the news was. Imminent, sudden death—her friend's or her own—had been as familiar to her as a lover from the first time she punctured her skin with a needle.

I said, "You two make a lot of money dealing?"

"You the government?"

"Hardly."

She was getting irritated. "Then what do you care?" she shouted. "Stop with all these questions and tell me."

"Curtis Hopkins is dead. Joseph Cantel killed him."

May Carter turned and stared at the apartment building, slowly turned back, crossed her arms and looked down at the

street. She said, "Shit," with no more emotion than if a traffic
light had turned yellow on her.

I said, "Why would Cantel kill him?"

"I don't know. I only met Cantel one time."

"When was that?"

"Few days ago I think."

"How long did Curtis know him?"

"Maybe a week."

"He say they didn't get along?"

"Not to me."

"Would Curtis rip off his connection?"

"He might. But not this soon."

"How'd they meet?"

"Friend of Curtis introduced them. Told Curtis this man
could provide him with as much stuff as he could handle."

"Who was this friend?"

"White hillbilly dude always wearin'a blue jean jacket,
blonde hair hangin' in his eyes."

"Stacey Ford?"

"I believe that's his name. Stacey Ford." She said it to herself
to see if it sounded familiar. "I didn't never know him, but Curtis knew him awhile and said he was all right. Personally, I don't
never trust hillbillies." She turned and looked at the apartment
again.

"I've got to inform the police there was a murder. You wanna
come with me or would you rather I give you some time to get
lost first?" She didn't answer. I said, "You can come with me and
tell me more about Cantel and Curtis."

"I told you I don't know nothin' about Cantel. I only met him
the one time. I only been stayin' with Curtis about a month. I
don't know much about him either. Police are gonna drop this
one on me, I know it. I'm the easiest one for it."

"They can't. I know Cantel killed him. Where'd you meet
Cantel?"

"Downtown."

"At the Midnight Lounge?"

She nodded. "In the basement. His office I guess."

"Come with me," I said. "I'll wait to call the police and I'll
drop you off wherever you want."

She looked at the building once more, then said, "Okay."

"You wanna get some things?"

She shivered violently. "I ain't goin' in there."

TWENTY

I headed for the Midnight Lounge. On the way, May Carter started to realize she was not only out a home but was going to have to scuffle for dope again. She whispered, "I can't keep anything permanent." I looked at her; the corners of her mouth quivered.

"Tell me about it."

"Nothin' to tell, except that's the second boy that died on me this year. Allan took a overdose in January right in front of my eyes. Now Curtis gets hisself murdered. Must be I'm a jinx."

"Kind of guys you hook up with don't require jinxes."

She said, "I've got to quit this life."

I hoped she meant life-style, but didn't say anything.

At the Lounge, I asked my friend the bartender if Cantel was back yet.

He answered, "Been back and left again."

"To where?"

"Cantel is *my* boss; he don't answer to me. All I know is I don't expect him back for a while."

"How long was he here?"

"Long enough to empty the safe in his office. Long enough to ask if anybody'd been in looking for him."

"You mention me?"

"No." He looked down quickly at the rag he wiped the counter with.

"Liar."

"He pays me, asshole. Besides, I didn't tell him you saw his office, only that you were in here asking after him."

"How do you know he emptied the safe?"

"He called me in there to ask a ton of questions, one of which was about you, and he had the safe open and was taking out bricks of money and stacking them in the suitcase."

"I never told you my name."

"I described you. He told me you were Kruger."

"How much money did he stack in the suitcase?"

"He told me once he had fifty grand stashed in case he had to vanish.

I whistled. "Fifty sittin' in a safe just in case?"

"I know. I always figured him to be inflating the amount. He talked like a bigshot when he had a snootful, but there was a lot of money in that suitcase. Lots of hundreds and twenties."

"What were some of the other questions?"

"Had I seen Stacey Ford today? Did I know how to get in touch with him? Did I know anything about him? Did I know anything about you?"

"He was loading money the whole time?"

"The whole time."

"You know anything about Ford?"

"Same as I know about you—nada."

"Ever meet the man?"

"I know who he is, period."

"Did you know Cantel was dealing heroin from his office?"

He was silent for five seconds, then said in a low voice, "I know they wasn't trading stamps down there. I figured that's what you wanted, tell you the truth. Just another junkie." He nodded at May who stood off by herself at the end of the bar watching the dancer on stage. He said, "That colored girl don't get high on life, Mac. I seen her in here day before yesterday with a sleazy lookin' black dude. They was downstairs with Cantel for a long time."

"Cantel never gets busted?"

"Never. He pays somebody, but I couldn't say who."

"Couldn't or wouldn't."

"Couldn't."

"Any Latin gangbangers ever come in here?"

"Not that I know of. We get plenty of Latins, but I wouldn't know about gangs."

"Any Latins go in back with Cantel?"

"Sure, all the time. Latins, whites, blacks, Asians, Martians for all I know. Every junkie in town's gotta be from somewhere."

We left. I started up Clark, on my way to Cantel's girlfriend's apartment. May was starting to hurt. She shook like a dog shitting razor blades even though she hugged herself tight and I had the heater on max. She didn't say anything, but when her teeth started clicking, I said, "You got a place around here you can cop?"

"I couldn't pay for a candy bar right now."

"I'll front you a bag just so I don't have to watch this."

We detoured to a two-flat on 26th. She ran up the stairs clutching two twenties. Came back out ten minutes later, calm-faced.

We drove to Ohio Street. May smoked my Kools one after the other and didn't say much except, "This dope ain't so hot." She said it three times because she probably forgot she'd said it before.

I told her it would be cheaper if she cultivated a "juice and beans" habit, which is cough syrup mixed with Doriden, or "Fours and Doors," Tylenol Number Four and Doriden. Both are cheap heroin substitutes, popular and easy to come by on the West Side and the maintenance costs are about a third of a junk habit.

She said contempuously, "I ain't no syrup-head and I won't ever be."

I said, "It's easier to cop than heroin and I read the high is comparable."

"The high is shit. And people die from too much of that just like they die from heroin."

"Be cheaper."

"A human being got to be low to settle for that. Curtis said he used to do 'T's and Blues' before they fucked up the Talwin with that shit that blocked the high. He says the high was garbage, plus some people laugh at you when they find out."

Even junkies have a pecking order.

I knocked long and hard on the apartment door even though I was certain nobody was home. May leaned against the wall next to the door, arms crossed tightly over her breasts. It seemed to be her natural stance cold or hot, high or hurting.

I worked on the lock with my passkey and celluloid card, finally got the door open.

The first room on the left side of a long hallway running away from the door was a bedroom. Huge bed with pink spread and pillows. Pale blue lounging furniture. The room looked ransacked, but I quickly realized that was the result of a hasty departure. There was an empty block of space on the floor of the closet, probably where suitcases had been stored, gaps in the hanging clothes, only a few pairs of shoes in the rack underneath the dresses. The four dresser drawers were open and empty except for some underwear draped over the sides.

I wandered through the five rooms hoping something would jump out at me like an open map with a town circled on it, but the girl probably didn't know anything. Cantel must've called her from his office, told her to be packed and ready when he got here.

In the kitchen, I found a key in a sugar can. I went outside the front door, told May to open up if the key didn't work, but it did. I went back inside, found some canceled checks and ripped open envelopes underneath some magazines on a table next to the bed. The girlfriend's name was Alice Baker.

May was following me through the apartment like a sleep-walker with chest pain. She didn't look at anything in particular, she stopped when I did, resumed moving when I did. She didn't know why we were here and wasn't interested enough to ask.

I said, "You need a place to crash?"

She blinked, looked at me, then at a picture on the wall. Said, "I guess I do."

"This apartment's vacant."

"Who lives here?"

"A woman named Alice Baker, but she won't be coming back for a while."

"I got friends I can stay with I think."

"Save 'em for a last resort. I'd let you stay at my place but I don't tell addicts where my place is let alone let them stay there. You can't hide out here forever, but I figure you got at least two days, maybe longer, before the police start looking for Baker. After a couple of days, stay away during the day, come back around midnight. Cops hardly ever come calling that late. The rent's probably paid. Anybody in the building asks you a question, tell 'em you're housesitting for Alice Baker who had to leave town suddenly. Tell them you two're best friends."

"She white?"

"Yeah."

"Maybe she's prejudiced and her neighbor's know it."

"So what? Tell 'em you're an exception. You saved her life once or something."

"Alice Baker?"

"That's right. I realize you'll hock everything you can carry out the front door, but Alice Baker has a rich boyfriend and he's rich because of people like you. So it'll only be poetic justice. Here's the key. Try not to lose it." I dropped it in her hand. "I'll be stopping by. I'll knock twice. If I phone, I'll ring twice, hang up and ring back. Anything happens or anybody calls and keeps calling, call this number." I gave her a card with my business number.

She'd kept with the junkie bewildered looks, so I wrote down exactly what I'd just said on a three-by-five card, stuck it down the front of her blouse inside her bra where she'd be sure to feel it when she woke up and take it out and look at it. She watched me do it, still looked confused, said nothing. I handed her the rest of my Kools, steered her to the bedroom, sat her down on the edge of the bed. I pushed her gently backwards. She flopped on her back.

"Now go to sleep," I said and left.

I went to a phone booth on the corner. Dialed 911 and said that a junkie-pusher named Curtis Hopkins had been murdered, gave the address. I thought for some seconds, debating whether to mention Cantel, decided to give May a break for a day or two. I cradled the phone.

TWENTY-ONE

Elvia Reyes was sitting on the front steps when I got home. I didn't notice her at first, but she said, "Dan?" when I turned up the walk and then I saw her sitting there, shivering, arms wrapped around her chest just like May.

She followed me into the apartment. I got a red flannel shirt from the closet, draped it over her shoulder and shoved her into the bathroom. Said, "Take a shower and put this on. I'll wash your clothes in the sink and hang 'em in the hallway."

She came out fifteen minutes later. The tails of the shirt covered half her thighs. The length of leg it didn't cover was as skinny as a bamboo stalk, making her feet look abnormally large. Her hair was combed straight back, the black parts glistening, shiny wet, the blonde parts looking dull and crinkly.

I sat on the living room couch drinking a Strohs and petting Bugs, staring at the news on TV but not paying attention. I had a beer on the table for Elvia. She sat next to me and started to sip from it.

I said, "So you're rich now, right?"

"Don't make fun of me. You knew he didn't have the money."

"You should of known it, too."

"I had to make sure."

"He kept looking at you like you were naked. He'd of told you anything to get you to go with him. You should listen to me if we're going to be partners."

"I got to take a chance on any leads come my way. People can call me stupid afterward if they want, but I'm taking chances. You have any of those pills you gave me the other night?"

I said, "When I get money, I cop Valium first, then I pay the rent." I handed her two, watched her swallow them with a gulp of beer.

She said, "How do you get so many of these?"

"I grew up with a guy who became a doctor. Three years ago,

I followed his wife to see if she was cheating on him and my fee was a Valium script whenever I ask."

"Isn't that against the law?"

"I would imagine, but I don't think he lies awake at night worryin' I'm gonna turn him in."

"Was his wife cheating?"

"Of course. How bad was Ford today?"

"He tied me up. Well, my hands he tied. To the end of the bed."

"He hurt you?"

"He didn't beat me if that's what you mean. I'd rather not talk about it."

"How long did you wait on the steps?"

"An hour."

"He drive you?"

"No. He fell asleep afterward. I worked my wrists loose then took every dollar he had on him and hired a cab a block away."

"How much did he have?"

"About three hundred dollars."

"You got it now?" I grinned, thinking of Ford waking up to empty pockets.

"Yep."

"Good."

She said, "All the way there, he kept saying he had the money, then when we got there he said he wanted sex first. Then he tied my hands to the end of the bed, pulled my jeans off and said, 'Guess what? I lied, chiquita,' and started to laugh like he was the cleverest man in the world. When I left, I wrote him a note that said 'Guess what? You're broke.'"

"Where'd he take you."

"An apartment on Halsted."

"House or complex?"

"Fairview Gardens. A big brick building. Old one."

"What apartment?"

"519 was on the door."

"His?"

"I don't think so. It was decorated like a woman's. Soft colors, you know? Pink, pale yellow. Lace on the drapes and stuff."

"He'll come looking for that money."

"Let him."

"He rape you the first time, too? At Mrs. Salazar's?"

"More or less. By the time I woke up—. My brother brought him there that time. He watched the whole time. Thought it was very funny. They were both real high. Another reason I wasn't so sad to hear my brother is dead."

"You want to call the police?" I knew she had to say no, but I asked anyway.

"Wetbacks don't call the police," she said. "And don't feel sorry for me. I can tell that look on your face. I'll get him sooner or later."

"I don't feel sorry for you, but I feel bad you went through what you did to find out what should of been obvious. It was useless, shouldn't of happened."

"It's maybe not nice to say, but I'd go through lots worse than that to get that money."

TWENTY-TWO

Elvia slept in my bed; I tried to sleep on the couch. At 4:00 A.M., I gave it up. I let Bugs out of his cage and serenaded him with blues licks on the SG. I didn't plug in to the amp, but Bugs digs blues in any form. When you've been dumped in a garbage can you know what it's like to be left behind.

At 8:00 A.M., I shook Elvia awake. She said she wasn't going anywhere and I told her to snooze all day if she needed, then made the bedroom as dark as I could.

Luis Santiago sat behind a gray metal desk cluttered with paper and file folders and notebooks. He wore a black suit, white shirt with burgundy tie, and the sincere toothy smile.

I said, "We gonna have a Latino mayor next year?"

He smiled larger. "I'm sorry about that speech I gave the other day."

"No problem."

"We're getting people registered. Slow but sure. It's kind of like chopping down a sequoia using a penknife. Takes forever, but when it goes there's going to be one hell of a crash. They'll hear it everywhere. You never called about the meeting with the Kings."

"Didn't have to. Three of 'em were waiting for me at my office after I left here. How well do you know those guys?"

"Not very. I've dealt with two or three, but they don't talk with people like me."

"Enrique Medina?"

Santiago frowned. "Yes, I know Enrique. I don't know, there's something about him. People follow him. Unfortunately he chooses to lead them off cliffs."

"Who follows him besides Romeo Kings?"

Santiago shrugged. "Why do you ask?"

"I've talked to him twice and I didn't notice any leadership charisma. You heard if any King came into some big money?"

"No."

"Any of them suddenly cut out for Mexico or vanish"—I snapped my fingers—"like that recently?"

"Not that I heard."

"Would you hear if it happened?"

"There'd be talk. It'd get to me."

"You told me the other day they push heroin. What kind of amounts and how long they been at it?"

"Sure they deal it. Scag, they call it. It's more than likely not enormous quantities like pills and pot, but—"

"But the clientele is very loyal, right?"

"You shouldn't joke about it, Dan. It's a tragic problem down here."

"I can't sit and cry over junkies I never met. I don't care that much anymore."

He said, "That's easy for you to say. I know too many."

"So do I. Those I don't joke about."

"You'd know a lot more of them if you worked down here. Each one I meet shaves another coat of varnish off. A lot of pain is underneath."

I said, "If I can't change something, I laugh at it. A hundred years from now, who's gonna care?"

Santiago was annoyed with me. He frowned again, started bouncing a pencil off the edge of his desk. "I wish it were that easy for me. If everybody felt like you where would we be?"

"Up shit creek."

"Precisely. You learn who killed Ricardo Reyes?"

"Not that I could prove."

"Will the police solve it?"

"I doubt it. I think it was a King. Or somebody who wanted witnesses to think it was a King. I'm at least trying to find out who. The police probably gave the file to a cadet and told him to check on it if he had the time. You know Stacey Ford? Tough little hillbilly with long blonde hair?"

"No."

"Joseph Cantel? Ex-fighter, owns the Midnight Lounge now."

"No."

"I hoped you did."

"They involved in Reyes' murder? I though you were centering on Orlando Finney and the Kings. And I thought you were interested in illegal aliens."

"I'm way beyond Finney and illegals. I'm up to murderers and heroin dealers and heroin addicts and a poverty-stricken Mexican girl who'd screw a leper on prime time TV to get her hands on a sack of money that probably doesn't even exist anymore."

He tugged at his shirt collar, a confused look on his face. "I'm not sure what you're talking about."

"I hoped you knew Cantel. He deals junk. Stacey Ford introduced him to me and I don't know why. The reason Ford gave turned out to be bogus. When Cantel found that out he got the willies, scooped up his girlfriend and split. Somehow Cantel ties in with Finney so I hoped you knew him so I could figure out how. That's my life—figure this, figure that."

Santiago grinned apologetically. "I'm not acquainted with every lowlife in Chicago, Dan. Not even every one in Pilsen."

"I'd enjoy finding someone who was."

"You still want that meeting with the Kings?"

"Nah, they always find me when they wanna talk. I still think one of them got the bag of money that disappeared when Ricardo Reyes got sliced. It's Orlando Finney's money, sort of, and the way they keep searching for him, I think they wanna kill him. If they do have the money, maybe they figure they got to because he'll be coming after them."

Santiago said, "They figure, you figure. Maybe you're both wrong."

"Would Finney go gunning for the Kings?"

"Only if their backs were turned. Listen, sorry I can't help."

"It's okay. Only thing is, I don't think there's anybody in Chicago who can."

"Go to the police. They can help."

"Not yet, Luis."

Santiago didn't say anything for a bit, then he said, "Dan, I know you do drugs. I know you're cynical and bitter about things. Maybe you think life is absurd, you wonder why bother. But heroin has to make you mad, too. It's not like the rest of these drugs. It's slavery."

I said, "Yeah, Luis, it does make me mad. Let's go up and down the street and tell these kids to just say no."

Across from Santiago's building was a newstand. Mostly Spanish languages newspapers and magazines, but they had a few copies of the *Sun-Times*. In the middle of the front page was a headline that said DRUG KILLINGS ON SOUTH SIDE—4 DEAD. I scanned it lazily until I saw Curtis Hopkin's name. I didn't recognize the last names of the other three, but the first names were Alton, Ed and Townsend. I recognized the first three and three out of four was good enough for me. I took the medicine bottle from my pocket and ate two Valium.

Joseph Cantel had killed all four people whose name and number he'd written on the paper in his office. And nobody knew he'd done it except me. It appeared to be in my best interests that he never find that out.

I was unsure what to do. I'm supposed to tell the police about murder, but I needed to know too much about things. The police would bully me and then proceed to forget about it if they didn't get Cantel pronto. Junkies and pushers killing each other. So what? For all I knew Cantel could drop completely out of sight. And this was a man who killed four people because he was *nervous*.

What would a paranoid bastard like that do to Goddamn-Dan-Kruger if he found out I'd ratted on him?

TWENTY-THREE

Driving north on Clark, I was trying to figure out what to do next, when I realized I wasn't the only person who knew Cantel had offed four pushers. If Stacey Ford had introduced Cantel to Curtis Hopkins, there was a very good possibility he'd been the middleman with the other three also. I wondered if Ford had seen a paper. If he had, he was probably as uptight as I was. I headed for the Fairview Apartments.

The building was a five story, Depression-era brick. Huge, boxlike, no frills. Also no security system except burglar bars on some of the first floor windows.

Room 519 was on the top floor. I knocked hard on the door, was surprised and apprehensive when it opened right away. It wasn't Ford, it was a woman. Thirtyish, plain looking, plump, a bottle blonde. Judging from the look on her face, she'd been around a city block more than once. It wore an expression of total boredom. She had on a tattered floor length yellow robe that she held together above and below the clasp in front of her stomach with her left hand. From the flashes of skin that peeked out, I could see the robe was all she had on.

I asked, "Is Stacey Ford here?"

She looked me up and down. Said, "I don't know any Stacey Ford. Why you think he's here?"

"Friend of mine visited him here last night."

"Your friend is mistaken."

I pulled out my wallet, opened it, took out a five and held it between us at chest level. She looked at it, eyes flickering a little. I said, "Southern guy with blonde hair, always wears a blue jean jacket and a white T-shirt. Never walks when he can run."

She shook her head no and leaned against the doorframe.

I said, "He could be in big trouble. Life or death type trouble. If you know where he is, I could warn him."

"But I don't know him so how could I know where he is?"

I looked behind her. I could see a corner of a room off the hallway that ran straight behind her. The colors in the room were green, yellow and pale pink. I said, "That'd be a good reason I gotta admit, but my friend described this place pretty well and she distinctly remembers the number. Where were you last night?"

"Working. I'm a waitress."

"Where?"

"You a census worker or something?"

"Yeah. I'm a census worker."

She smiled a tiny smile.

I said, "See, if you were working, they could of had a real ball going on here."

"Listen, what if I do know Ford? I'm not saying I do, understand? But if I did, people don't appreciate other people revealing things about them they don't want known. Some people get mad about things like that."

"I understand that. Ordinarily I wouldn't be so pushy about it, but like I said, this could be a matter of life and death. Before now, I'd go to The Dangerous Game and wait for him, but I don't think he'll be in a regular hangout after what happened yesterday."

She thought for some seconds, then reached suddenly for the five with the hand that held the robe together. The robe parted and I received a full frontal show. She left the robe open for a few seconds before she lazily pulled the two sides together again. She smiled coyly. "It'll cost you ten for the show, five for the info."

"Ten bucks? No offense, ma'm—"

"Vicki, with an 'i.'"

"No offense, Vicki, but I can go to Puss 'n Booths or Little Bo Peep and see that much for a buck. Plus they'll dance a little."

"Yeah, but this is more personal like, more private. Besides, you don't pay for the show, you don't get the info."

I worked out two more fives handed them over.

She said, "You Dan Kruger by any chance?"

"Might be."

She laughed. "Then don't worry about finding Stacey. He'll find you. You and the spic broad."

"Yeah?"

She smiled, didn't say anything.

"You got any idea where he is right now?"

"Go home. He's probably waiting for you."

I drove to Fremont like an immigrant taxi driver, laying on the horn, ignoring yellow lights, rolling stop signs. I was scared to death what I'd find there. Elvia beat up or dead, Bugs dead, the house ransacked. The Valium wasn't doing much to calm me as I envisioned the worst.

When I turned the corner from Addison onto Fremont, I saw Ford's beat up yellow Chevy parked in front of the apartment. He was inside the car.

I parked behind him. We both got out and met at the front of my car.

"Where's Elvia?" he asked.

"You wanna rape her again?"

He smirked. "Nobody has to rape that Mex, my friend. She's saying I raped her? That's good."

"She implied it wasn't the first time. She'll put up with a ton of crap for that money. Lots more than most people."

"The bitch cleaned me out," he yelled, flinging his arms out. "Down to my last dime."

"Justice, Ford. You need dough, go hit up Vicki."

His eyes narrowed. "How'd you know about Vicki?"

I smiled.

"That Mex bitch. She's been here telling you bullshit stories like how she got raped. Get my money back."

"Why should I?"

"It's mine. I need it."

"You wouldn't be planning to blow town?"

"Why would I wanna do that?"

"Curtis Hopkins?"

"Who's that?"

"You're a bad liar. I met Hopkins yesterday. A real laid back dude. I met another person who told me you and Hopkins were pals." I needed to be careful about what I said. I didn't want to tell anybody I knew Cantel had murdered the four dealers. I didn't know who Cantel was still talking to. Ford maybe suspected the same thing I did, but I'd let him wonder if I suspected the same thing he did.

Ford clasped his hands behind his neck and worked his head around, stretching muscles, trying to calm himself down. Softly he said, "Kruger, what're you trying to say?"

"I've been wondering who you work for, Ford. I can't tell. I'm not sure you even know. But after what happened yesterday I see you're a scared man. Join the club."

"What happened yesterday?"

"Don't play me for a moron, Ford."

"I just need my money, man." His hand came down. He fumbled in his jean jacket pocket, got out a pack of Marlboros, lit up.

I said, "It's not yours anymore. Possession is nine-tenths of the law. Least that's what I keep hearing."

"I don't know what that skinny slut told you, but she took my money last night. I want it."

"How do I know it's yours? Describe it."

"Goddamit, Kruger, you are pissing me off." He threw the cigarette at my feet and came at me, swinging. A left caught me on the side of my face. A solid punch that shivered my jaw.

I went down, he fell on top of me, throwing short jab-like punches. I blocked most of them, but the ones that got through hurt like hell. I lifted up and twisted sideways, trying to roll him over. We bucked and twisted and flailed in the street like a couple of drunken old hookers arguing over a two dollar john.

I heard a door slam and seconds after that Stacey Ford wasn't on top of me anymore. He was on his back next to me in the street and Elvia was straddling him. Ford didn't have a chance. Elvia was a blur as she screamed and punched and clawed and spit and poured out torrents of Spanish at him, her hair whipping back and forth, up and down.

Ford was covering up and shouting, "Goddamit!" and "Shit!"

and "Christ!" but that was about all he could do. I got Elvia pulled off him on the third try. I pushed her toward the house, but she resisted, so I stopped when we were ten feet away. I looked at Ford over my shoulder. He stood up slowly. Elvia's fingernails had made long scratches on each side of his face. Bubbles of blood were growing in the ripped skin. His face was as wet as a swimmer's from her saliva.

He ran the back of his hand across his face, wiping away the blood and spit, then pointed at Elvia. Said, "Give me my money, cunt."

She spat at him. Most of it landed on my shoulder. She tried to push me away so she could get at him. She was one feisty girl.

I said, "Somebody around here has called the law by now. Let's bet what they decide is worse, rape or picking pockets."

He stood there a bit, hate and blood on his face, then walked quickly to his car. When he was inside he rolled down the window, yelled, "I'll get the both of you I swear." He squealed away.

Elvia and I looked at each other. She was wearing only a white David Bowie T-shirt of mine above slim white panties. I was getting an eyeful this morning. Then I started to laugh. I said, "I was scared to death for you all the way here. It's Ford I shoulda been worried for."

She looked angry for a second, then a grin broke through and she laughed too, tossing her hair out of her face.

I said, "You and I got a knack of making enemies, girl. No wonder we're partners. We'll have the whole town and half of Mexico after our butts before long."

TWENTY-FOUR

I was wrong about the cops thing. Nobody called them. In my neighborhood nobody calls the cops unless something serious happens. Like when I turn up my stereo too loud.

When we got back inside, Elvia went to the bathroom and I heard water from the shower pepper the mat. When she was done, she went into the bedroom to dress. The whole time I sat on the couch, Bugs beside me, strumming jazz chords on the SG. Not playing any songs, just noodling. I thought for a bit more, then talked loudly so Elvia could hear me in the other room. I said, "The three of us are going to leave here. Stay somewhere else for a while."

She walked into the living room, dressed again in the acid washed jeans and black sweater, feet bare, her head tilted to the left side as she combed her still damp hair. The comb flipped drips of water to the floor. "Three of us?"

"You, me and Bugs."

"Why?"

"Because people keep showing up here. People I don't want to see because most of them consider me a walking punching bag."

"Where do we go?"

"Don't know yet."

"Why do the people keep coming here?"

"In the yellow pages, I advertise my home address and phone so I can attract clients who for one reason or another wouldn't want to see me at the office. The flip side of that is when I get mixed up in a mess like this any yahoo can look me up in the phone book and find out where to go to fuck with me any hour of the day."

"But we need a place to go."

"If Marvin wasn't so mad at me, we could crash there."

"Does he fall for women easy?"

"Marvin thinks he's Errol Flynn."

"Then let me talk to him." She smiled slyly.

"I don't know if it'll help, Elvia. He's never been this mad at me. He was so scared, he's probably embarrassed about it now. That'll make him even madder."

"Do we *have* to stay away from here?"

I didn't want to tell her about Cantel. I just said yes.

"Then let me talk to him."

I put Bugs in his traveling cage, poured fresh water in the plastic clip-on bottle on the side of it. I filled a grocery bag with bunny paraphernalia—a ten pound bag of litter, cardboard litter box, bunny chow, two heads of romaine lettuce. In another bag, I placed three pairs of jeans, clean socks, and three black T-shirts. I filled two medicine bottles. One with one hundred whites, the other with one hundred Valium. Stuck both bottles in my windbreaker pocket.

I looked around the room. Decided I wanted the SG with me. I gave both bags to Elvia, went to the other side of the room and laid the SG in its case. Holding Bugs in his cage in my left hand, and the SG in its case in my right hand, I led Elvia to the Skylark. I felt like a fleeing war refugee forced to abandon my home, not knowing what would be left when I returned.

It occurred to me this would be something to worry about only if I actually did return.

TWENTY-FIVE

In the small parking lot in front of the office, a uniform cop was waiting for me in a Ford Cutlass. The car had no plates and no "Applied For" sticker in the window. I knew he was waiting for me because I'd come to expect that anybody loitering outside my living or working areas was waiting for me. Waiting for someone else just wasn't done these days.

I parked next to the Cutlass. When I opened the door, the cop leaned toward the half down passenger window and said, "You Kruger?"

I nodded.

He leaned back and pointed to the seat next to him. He had a striking but not handsome dark complexioned face—like if Tony Danza had had his mug rearranged with a baseball bat. Wide flat nose, lips too thick, protruding jaw, an indented forehead.

Elvia got out and we looked at each other over the roof of the Skylark. The cop leaned toward us again and said, "Tell the chiquita to beat it for now. It's okay." His voice was a smooth, pleasant, almost jovial tenor. A major part of any cop's job is conning civilians into doing or saying things they don't want to do or say, and this guy must've long ago learned the most effective way to do that is to come off as your average kind-hearted Joe.

Elvia said, "I'll talk to your friend," and walked inside.

I slid in, took a quick look at the cop's chest. No badge, which probably meant he didn't want me knowing his number. No plates, no window paper, no badge, no number. He wasn't here to chat.

I suddenly became very aware of the pills in my pocket. And the bag of pot in the glove compartment of the Skylark. The pills and pot have been such an integral part of my life-style for so long that they don't seem illegal to me anymore. Stupid, I know, but I tend to equate them with food, air and water. Essential ingredients with which to joust with life. But sometimes it flashes on me that these ingredients can put a man in jail—or at least cost him a good chunk of change. This was flashing on me intensely right now as I sat holding amphetamines next to a cop who wasn't planning to get very friendly.

When I closed the door, the cop said, "I bring a message from Joe."

"What Joe? Joe Blow? Joe Stalin? I know a lot of Joe's."

"Shut up, Kruger. Why do all you PI's run around pretending to be fucking Henny Youngman?"

"You're right. I'll be good."

"This is a Joe you met recently."

My stomach went cold. I said, "Oh, that Joe." The homicidal maniac Joe. I put a Kool in my mouth. Sucked long when I lit it.

He was watching me close. "Yeah, that Joe. That Joe says you better forget you met him. You better forget everything you know about him. You better forget everything you learned about him. Forget he hired you and forget the name of the establishment he hired you in. Forget—"

"I get the picture. Joe wants me to forget about Joe. This Joe's message, or yours?"

"I'll word it like this. Joe's message is my message and vice versa. Joe has lots of friends in this town. You're not one of them, which means you are automatically dog puke in my eyes. And just in case you happen to be one of those private dicks who likes to think he's only slightly less official than a real cop and that's going to help you out should you get your pecker caught in a vise, let me set you straight on that. To me—to most real cops—you ain't a damn bit different from any other scumbag in this town. Fuck up and you are dead meat." It was bizarre hearing this talk coming from such a pleasantly pitched voice. It was like if MacNeil and Lehrer decided to have a cursing war on their Report.

I said, "You delivering a message or trying to scare me out of town?"

He smiled a tight, humorless smile. "Take it how you like, Dannyboy. Just remember that if you fuck up and you and I have to talk about it, one of us wears a badge and one of us don't."

"How do I know you wear a badge? Show me."

The smile was briefly genuine. "When you see my badge you will know you are in the deepest of troubles."

I said, "Where is Joe? Did he tell you about the bag of money?"

The smile was gone and a flicker of interest flashed across his eyes. Joe hadn't told him shit about any bag of money. But all the cop said was, "Out!"

"Why couldn't Joe give me this message himself? I got a phone. Hell, I got two phones."

He reached past me, yanked the door handle down hard, shoved the door open. "Get the fuck out of my fucking car, fuckhead!" he yelled.

He was a genuine Chicago cop all right.

I stood next to the Skylark, shaking my head, smoking another Kool when Elvia came out. She was smiling that smile that made her face look sliced in half. She said, "We can stay at your friend's house. I fixed it. What did the policeman want?"

I said, more to myself than her, "Joseph Cantel, the heroin man, has a cop working for him and the cop doesn't care who knows it."

"Is that trouble?"

"I'd say so."

"For us?"

"For us."

"But we can hide at your friend's."

"Not now."

What was left of the wide smile dropped away.

I said, "I appreciate the job you did in there on Marvin, but it just dawned on me that if they find me here and at home, they can find Marvin here and at home. And if they find Marvin, they find us. I can't get Marvin into any more trouble than he's already in. He *is* my best friend. And if I get him any more scared than he already is, *he* might hire somebody to chill me. No, we'll find a hotel. A cheap, out of the way one."

"What about the bag? We going to look for it today?"

"Elvia, what do I have to do to explain this to you? Right now I'm more concerned with keeping healthy than in finding that damn bag. We aren't quitting, we're just making sure we don't get killed doing it."

She got mad. "Are you afraid of these scum?"

"Of course."

"Cheesh."

I ticked on my fingers. "Finney, Ford, a Latino street gang, a heroin dealer"—I didn't mention the heroin dealer had killed four people the previous afternoon—"and now a cop so crooked he don't care if I know he's crooked. He only cares about me not knowing his name so he can come at me unannounced if he needs to. I've been in this business long enough to know when to get scared. Right now I'm good and scared. Did you see Ford before you jumped him today? Even Ford is scared and he's a tough nut."

"You're all just chickenshit."

"There seems to be a lot of drugs involved here and these new breed drug types start blasting first and don't even think about asking questions later. They make the Mafia look like the FBI. We'll still work on finding the bag, but first we find a place we can go to sleep without worrying about whether we'll wake up. You sticking with me or no?"

She stared at the cement for a few seconds. Said, "Yeah, I'll stay with you, but I think you're acting too rashly. Going overboard, you know?"

"Always take safe over sorry. Kruger's words to live by."

I asked Elvia to wait in the Skylark, then went inside to talk to Marvin. I wanted to get that over with.

He had his feet crossed on the desk, was idly thumbing through a *Hustler*. He didn't acknowledge me. He wore his usual uniform—dark slacks, white shirt, red and yellow power tie, gray socks and burgundy tasseled loafers. Such a proper insurance salesman. I wondered what our reaction to each other would be if we were to meet for the first time today instead of when we were thirteen. Both of us would probably curl our lips and walk in the opposite direction fast as we could go. Me muttering, "Yuppie twit," him thinking, "Derelict zero."

I cleared my throat, said, "So am I outta here?"

He didn't look up. "No, but you're real close."

"I'm glad. I like it here."

"You mean you can't beat the rent."

"Maybe I mean that, but maybe I don't. I'm sorry they came here and I can't promise they won't again."

"There's very few things a person can promise another person in this life." Normally I crack wise when Marvin starts philosophizing, but I shut up now. He turned a page, said, "You poking the Mex girl?"

"She's a client."

"That's not an answer."

"You shouldn't of asked the question. I know we're friends, but—" I rubbed my hands on my shirt, said, "The answer is no. Just a client."

"Too bad. Well, if you aren't, then while the two of you are staying at my place, I might be able to build some cultural bridges. So to speak." He finally looked up at me, smiled and winked.

"We can't stay with you. That's what I came in to tell you. I wanted to apologize for yesterday and thank you for the offer, but we have to go elsewhere."

He looked disappointed. "Why not? I just told her—"

"You want those Romeo King JD's waiting for you on your front porch some night?"

He didn't say anything, but the look on his face told me he hadn't thought about that. He'd been thinking only one thing when Elvia had been slinking around the office, smiling and purring. I said, "I'll call you from wherever we end up and give you a phone number so you can reach me in an emergency."

"One of these days, you'll have to break down and buy yourself an answering machine."

"One of these days I will. I'll call you through the day and you can give me messages, okay? Anybody calls for me, you tell 'em things got so hot for me I split and you don't know where. That should keep 'em out of your hair." I leaned against the door and we looked at each other for a second. I said, "You know, Marvin, you very often go above and beyond the call. And I guess you don't get a lot out of this relationship."

"Hey, don't forget the hundred twenty five a month. And this set up gives me a daily opportunity to say 'there but for the grace of God.'" He made a face. "And God knows that's something money can't buy."

"Maybe I could buy a life insurance policy. Kind of even things out a bit."

We both laughed. It was a standing joke. I couldn't afford his cheapest policy and I'd probably flunk the physical so bad they'd accuse Marvin of trying to insure a corpse. But, doctor, this man's dead.

I said, "By the way, how did Elvia con you into letting us stay over?"

"She implied she and I could build those cultural bridges."

"I wondered why the disappointment."

"What's her story? She never blushed or even blinked."

Poor sheltered Marvin. I said, "Using and being used are second nature to her. Where she's from, where she is now, it's a way of life. Plus right now she's on what she considers a mission. She'd promise anything, do anything, put up with anything, put herself or you or me through anything to get something she believes is hers."

"Sounds like not a good person to get hooked up with."

"It might pay well."

"Hope so. Then I can raise your rent." As I opened the door, he said, "Tell her that if improving Latin-Gringo relations is important to her, all she has to do is call."

I said, "I'll surely tell her, Marvin."

TWENTY-SIX

Another chilly April mist was leaving water bubbles on everything as I drove north, wipers on slow. I saw a few small hotels but kept going. The one I picked was a rooming hotel on a side street just off Howard Street, almost in Evanston. It was in a Caribbean neighborhood and was small, old, cheap, not clean and the only amenities were a room key, two chips of perfumed soap and two towels with a different name on them than the sign out front. But the location was prime. Even if they learned where we were, this far north the Romeo Kings would need a guide to find us.

Our room had saggy twin beds, a frayed easy chair and a nineteen inch color TV that had been new about the time Elvia was born. I smuggled Bugs up by putting a blanket from the trunk over his cage. Carried it under my arm like it was a suitcase. Soon as I lifted the cage door, he hopped out and commenced casing the room just like a bunny PI ought to. He found the wooden leg of the chair to his liking, started to gnaw.

By this time, Elvia was into big time sulking. We were making no progress finding "her" money, and on top of that, it appeared her partner was more interested in saving his neck than getting rich. She couldn't have been more correct.

I told her I needed to eat. If she wanted, she could join me, if not, fine. She followed me silently down the stairs and next door to a twelve-stool coffee shop. I asked if lunch was on Stacey Ford. She said no, so it was cheeseburgers, french fries, and coffee. When there is danger ahead, I stoke up on grease and caffeine. Elvia was heavily into her pouting mood, shrugging her shoulders or muttering "yes" or "no" when I asked a direct question, like did she enjoy her sandwich or was she as sick of gray sky and rain as I was.

I decided on Valium for dessert. I shook out two for me then tilted the bottle at Elvia.

She scowled. "I don't want those anymore. They make people lazy."

"Elvia, you cut me to the quick." I swallowed the two pills with a sip of lukewarm coffee. "You got to be lazy once in a while. People need to unwind."

"I can't now. If you weren't so nervous, you wouldn't want to either."

I started to feel peeved myself. Nobody enjoys having their sensible precautions interpreted as cowardice. I said, "This is like the Holy Grail to you."

She looked away. She wasn't sure what that meant and she didn't care enough to find out.

I called Marvin from a pay phone in the coffee shop. He told me Finney had called five minutes after I walked out the door. And five minutes after that, Enrique Medina had walked in the door. Both needed to talk to me.

I asked, "They sound angry?"

"They sounded Spanish."

"You tell them I got spooked and split?"

"Yeah."

"And?"

"Well, nobody's sittin' here waiting for you. The gangbanger chuckled when I told him."

"Another scaredygringo."

"Probably. Finney sounded like he hadn't been doing much chuckling about anything lately."

"Little tense, was he?"

"More than a little."

"This demonstrates the wisdom I've accrued over the years

as an investigator. I knew just when to take it on the lam. Was
Medina alone?"

"No, the guy with the roadmap face was with him."

"They didn't start in on you?"

"Nope."

"I wonder if that's good or bad."

"You asshole."

I laughed. "You know what I mean."

He gave me the phone numbers that Finney and Medina had
left with him.

Fear had become the dominant emotion in this case. Everybody seemed to be suffering a constant anxiety attack. Finney
had succumbed early on, which meant maybe he knew a little
more about what was going on. I called him first.

Soon as I said my name, he croaked, "Call them off." His
voice was strained and husky.

From the sound of it, he was way past anxiety. Bypassed fear
and gone straight to panic. The race down Lincoln Ave. with a
car of tough boys on his rear bumper must have prompted him
to reevaluate the whole affair and he obviously did not enjoy
what he came up with.

I said, "Call who off?"

"Those fucking animals that are out to kill me."

"You mean the Kings?"

"Who else?"

I laughed. "*Me* call them off? That's humorous, Finney. I snap
my fingers, the Kings jump."

"I went to your office the other day. They were parked down
the street."

"It's a free country. They can park where they want."

"Yeah, but they were parked there."

"In a court of law, that'd prove I control them all right."

"You don't work for them?"

"I do have a *few* moral boundaries. Very few and often nebu-
lous, but they're there." There was silence for some seconds. I
said, "You calling from Parkside Ave.?"

More silence.

"Well?"

"I'm going to kill Stacey Ford. Only he knew that address."

"You'll be at the end of a long line. Did Ford work for you?"

He ignored the question. Said, "You still hanging out with that Mex bitch who stole my money?"

"Yeah." I quickly added, "She's my client." Why was I so defensive about that?

"Then you haven't found the money?"

"Not yet. That's not my main priority right now."

Finney said, "Mine neither. You talk regular to the Romeo Kings?"

"Not very regular. Only when they wanna talk to me. I'm supposed to call the head boy after this conversation."

"Medina?"

"Medina."

"Square me with him."

"How?"

"I don't care how," he shouted. "Tell them to get off my back, dammit—"

Suddenly the sound of a jackhammer clattered through the phone. It was so near to where Finney was it drowned out his words. When it stopped I said, "Finney, where are you? Sounds like you're using a car phone on the Dan Ryan."

"Never mind where I am." He was still yelling. I moved the phone a few inches from my ear. "You tell that guy I could cause everybody trouble were I to start talking. Tell him if I haven't talked yet, it's obvious I won't talk unless I'm forced to. But they have got to give me a break."

"I think that's just what they wanna do. Starting with your neck."

"It's not funny."

"You got to take the point of view into account. What is it you can talk about?"

"That's none of your business."

"Who's 'everybody'?"

"Forget that. The message is for them, not you. Medina'll know what I'm talking about. Just tell him, okay?"

"Say pretty please."

"Dammit, Kruger, someday you're gonna need a favor."

"It'll be one bleak day when I need a favor from you. What you can talk about, it have anything to do with illegal aliens?"

Exasperated, he said, "I told you I don't traffic in *mojados*."

"Stop it, Finney. It's not like I'm trying to verify it. Everybody in town knows you smuggle IA's. I'm not gonna call immigration. With everything going on, you honestly think I give a shit about somebody hustling wetbacks?"

There was a pause again. Then he said, "It's got nothing to do with *mojados*."

"How about heroin?"

"What?"

"Joseph Cantel?"

"Dammit."

"You owe him money?"

"Maybe."

"Might be a good idea to pay up. If you can find him. He hired me to locate you. He's not a happy man."

Finney didn't talk.

I said, "Your friend Stacey Ford again. He conned Cantel into hiring me to flush you out. And the whole time Ford knew where you were. He drove me to the Midnight Lounge himself. He didn't say too many complimentary things about you, I'm afraid. He hinted to Cantel and me you were going to stiff your debts and get lost."

"That hillbilly son-of-a-bitch."

I was smiling, felt like laughing. "You still see Ford?"

"Not since when we went to your office and found them animals waiting for us. That redneck tried to set me up."

"I'm shocked. He has such an honest face. And you all adhere to such a high code of ethics."

Finney said, "You still working for Cantel then?"

"No. He got upset about something and left town."

"He's a violent man with a hair trigger temper. Plus he's loco. When he gets a mad on, run for it. That's sincere and honest advice. I know the man."

I said, "It's odd, well not so odd considering, but all the principles in this affair are diving for cover. You, me and Elvia, Joseph Cantel, now Ford wants to blow town. Everybody's scattering like elk at a lion's water hole. Except for the Kings. They're too tough—or too stupid."

"I doubt stupidity is the reason."

"I doubt it, too."

He said, "There's other people who aren't running away."

"Like who?"

He hesitated, then said, "Never mind."

I said, "Why don't you split town?"

"Cause the Mex bitch stole all my goddamn money, that's why. Is she with you now?"

"She's here, but she's giving me the silent treatment. I'm too chicken for her."

"Let me talk to her."

I yelled, "Elvia!" and held the phone in the air. She walked over slowly. When I handed her the receiver, I said, "Finney." She winced, put it to the side of her face.

I leaned against the plastic privacy side of the booth and put my ear close to the receiver. The conversation was in Spanish and Elvia didn't say much more to Finney than she'd been saying to me. Sounding small through the earpiece, Finney's voice was steady and fast. Elvia replied in a monotone voice with short sentences and frequently just one word. I had no idea what they were saying, but a pleading tone sounds the same in Spanish or English, and Finney was doing some major league pleading. He should have saved his breath. Elvia was refusing him out of hand. But Orlando Finney was going down for the third time, and like a drowning man, he was ready to settle for the slenderest of straws. After two minutes, Elvia looked at me, rolled her eyes and shook her head. She handed me the phone and whispered, "Tell him to go fuck himself." She walked back to the table.

I put the receiver to my ear. Finney was still talking Spanish, unaware Elvia had walked away. I let him continue for a bit. Hoped he'd say a name or a word or a phrase or a place I'd recognize. Come on Finney, give me a lead. But it was just nonsense to me. So I said, "Forget it, Finney. She's fifty feet away. There anything you wanna tell me?"

"I already did."

"What were you begging Elvia for?"

The jackhammer started chugging again. Over it, Finney shouted, "Fuck you, Kruger."

"Likewise Finney." I hung up.

I walked to our table. Still standing, I lit a Kool and said, "What'd he want?"

"My money." She stared into her coffee cup.

"What else?"

The shrug again.

"Being partners and all I thought we were supposed to tell each other everything. Your idea, if you remember."

She shrugged again.

I said, "Let me call Medina and then we'll look for your money."

She looked quickly up at me, her face changing from frowns and anger to smiles and delight. It was as sudden and dramatic as when the sun bursts through a stormy November sky.

TWENTY-SEVEN

I dialed Medina's number. Judging from the background noise, half of Pilsen must've been in the building celebrating something. They passed the phone around like it was a hookah. From one voice after another I got, "Whaddaya want?" "Who do you want?" "Oh, Medina," then gales of laughter. I said my name ten times to ten different people. Kept expecting to hear "Dan Kruger's not here" in reply.

Medina finally came on the line and said, "I talked to your yuppie friend in the white shirt this morning. I hope it was nothing I did to make you run away."

I smiled which was easy to do with Medina on the other end of a phone call. I said, "You've been the perfect gentleman, Enrique."

"I thought big tough private eyes never got scared."

"Big tough ones probably don't. But don't flatter yourself, it's just you guys. I haven't met anybody lately looking to start up a Dan Kruger fan club. I just now talked to Orlando Finney and—"

Medina interrupted. "Where is he?"

"Wouldn't say. Nobody wants to be anywhere anymore. But he would appreciate it if you 'fucking animals' would get off his back and leave him alone."

"Fucking animals?" Medina said it slow, incredulous.

"His exact words."

Medina chuckled unhumorously into the line. He said, "That's funny coming from a whore-beating faggot pimp, who on the side deals wetbacks like they're wheelbarrows."

"I suspected you'd get a kick out of it. He's petrified. He's so out of it he thought I was working for you."

"Like the Kings can't handle their own problems?"

"I think his mind has come unhinged from fear," I said. That chase down Lincoln Wednesday created too much stress for the man. I've heard and observed that Finney doesn't back down too often, but he's scared to death of you. Or maybe it's that respect you like to talk about."

Medina said, "Why don't you come down here so we can talk?"

"I was under the impression that's what we're doing."

"I can't talk business over this phone. It's probably tapped, plus there's nine thousand *pendajo's* wandering around who could listen in."

"Where's 'here'?"

"Pilsen. We got a safe house on 18th Street."

"Get real, Medina. I'll meet you, but not in a safe house on 18th Street in Pilsen. You can be uncomfortable for once. Discover how I've been feeling lately."

"You don't trust me?" He sounded genuinely wounded.

"Not one iota. There's a restaurant on the North Side called Barkers. I'll be there at five o'clock. You wanna talk to me, be there."

TWENTY-EIGHT

It was almost three o'clock. After caging and feeding Bugs, Elvia and I got in the Skylark and headed south on Broadway. She was talking a blue streak now. We were good friends again. I told her we had to stop and visit a friend of mine.

"Does your friend have anything to do with the money?" she asked suspiciously. She was getting to know me too well.

"Kind of. Finding 'your' money is going to involve doing a lot of little things here and there. Things that might seem unconnected. A lot of little questions asked. Stuff like that. Maybe we'll get lucky. It was cash so I doubt we'll find all of it." I didn't bother to tell her what I really believed. That the more time went by, the more I figured it would be a miracle on a par with the '69 Mets if we found any of it. The only reason I could think of that whoever stole it hadn't blown town or gotten it cleaned up so he could use it was that the person might be as scared as the rest of us. That person might not want to say or do anything to indicate he had just come into a large amount of dollars. So it was just possible the bag still sat somewhere. And just possible was good enough at the moment.

But I wanted to lay some groundwork for the unthinkable. I said, "If worse comes to worse, when do you decide to call off the hunt?"

"I don't understand."

"When do you say I quit? Decide it's hopeless." She looked at me, uncomprehending. I said, "You might conclude this money is more trouble than it's worth."

"What could be more trouble than money is worth?"

"Long knife slices, multiple bullet holes, thugs waving tire irons or clubs around."

"Those things aren't more trouble to me. We've been over this. You think I'm joking all the time? You think I make up how poor I was growing up? You think—"

I put up my hand, sighed. Said, "I realize you haven't been joking."

"Should I get a new partner? You want to quit?"

I said, "No and sometimes."

May let us in, then walked unsteadily to the sofa in Alice Baker's living room. The TV was on with the sound off. All drapes were closed, all lights off. The TV painted May and the couch a ghostly blue-gray. I sat next to her, looked her over. A glassy sheen dulled her eyes, her face was haggard. I couldn't tell if she recognized me, she didn't say anything at all.

I tossed her a pack of Kools, then opened the bottle of 20/20 I'd bought at Larry's Liquors a block from the apartment building. May lit a cigarette and after I tested for quality, drank a third of the bottle in one greedy swallow. She got up fast and stumbled to the hallway, gagging, both hands sealing her mouth. Retching sounds came from further inside the apartment.

I looked at Elvia who stood at the end of the sofa. Said, "Junkie."

Disgust clouded her face. She said, "Junkies puke more than they breathe." Elvia had seen such things often enough she didn't feel much compassion anymore either.

My card was on the armrest. When May came back I said, "Why didn't you call me?"

"Didn't have nothin' to say." Her voice was soft as a kitten's meow. She lay down and resumed staring at the game show on TV. She put the bottle to her lips and sipped this time.

"Anybody knock on the door?"

"No."

"Any phone calls?"

"That phone was ringing off the hook this morning."

"Answer it?"

"First time I did. I forgot. I told the party it was a wrong number. After a while, I took it off the hook. I got sick of the ringing. It was driving me nuts."

I hurried to the phone on the other side of the room. It was still unhooked. I set the handset back in the cradle. Said, "Not a good idea, May. People call over a long period of time and keep gettin a busy signal, they start to worry and have the phone company check it out."

"Let 'em, I don't care."

I doubted she cared about much of anything, except scoring junk. This woman was the only person who knew I knew Joseph Cantel had murdered someone. Why I'd opened my mouth I did not know. A junkie's philosophy of life could be summed up with 'fuck it.' Not a good person to share a scary secret with.

I said, "Was it a man or woman who called the first time?"

"Man."

"What'd he want?"

"I never asked."

Still looking at the TV she said, "If you give me thirty dollars, I'll make a call. I'll be better then."

"Valium help?"

"Valium don't do shit for me."

"Speed?"

"The only up I do is base. You got coke we can cook?"

"No."

I turned and looked at Elvia. She shook her head.

I said, "Give it up. I'll pay it back."

Elvia dug cash from her pocket, staring rage at me the whole time. May made two calls, talked brief and urgent, slammed the handset both times. After the third call, she set it down gently.

I said, "Will they bring it here?"

"I didn't just order no pepperoni pizza."

"Need a ride?"

"I'm gonna meet him at a stop on the L. This dude wouldn't want no strangers knowing his crib. He's plenty paranoid."

"You coming back here?"

"I think so. I like this place."

"Remember what I said. Another day or so and you might have some law stopping by."

"I ain't lettin' nobody in."

"They won't be asking please."

Just then the phone rang. The three of us looked at it like it was a cow talking. Elvia said, "Dan?" Her face was confused and angry because she didn't know anything about what May and I were talking about or why we were here or why she was paying for a junkie's fix.

The phone kept ringing.

I should've ignored it, but a professional PI is most of all a snoop. Curiosity grew with each bleep. After the tenth one, it swelled over and I picked up the receiver.

A male voice said, "Miss Baker?"

I said, "Alice isn't here now." I pitched my voice higher than normal and whispered, trying to sound like I was half asleep. I hoped the man would think I was Joseph Cantel.

"Is this Mr. Cantel?" I was in luck.

"Yeah."

There was a pause. The man wasn't so sure so I said, "Well?" I didn't want him to start thinking.

He said, "I've only had time to conduct a brief background sketch on the two individuals you're interested in. No time for surveillance, but I interviewed neighbors, co-workers, and the police. A preliminary background we call it. You might be interested to know they're both well known to the police."

The man was talking like a private cop. I said, "And?"

"Okay. This Dan Kruger *is* a private investigator. North Side. Strictly small potatoes. I can vouch for that because I never heard of the man and I know all the big-time operatives in town." He was reading off a paper and eating at the same time so he was pausing to chew or swallow after each sentence. "He was a squad car cop on the South Side a long time ago. Quit after he winged a colored kid during a robbery. Then he was a musician, can you beat that? From cop to guitar player? Now he's a PI. Not highly ethical, but not exactly crooked. I mean, he won't kill a spouse or fence hot jewelry like some small-timers, but for the correct amount of cash he'll do just about anything else. And the correct amount of cash is mighty low. I talked to a cop out of Wentworth who knows him. The cop says Kruger is a decent enough dick, but he has a drug problem, which sometimes causes him to be a bit slow on the uptake. We're not talking hard drugs here. No smack or coke or boat. No needles. But he's heavy into pills and booze and pot. And we all know how years of chemical abuse can get the old brain plenty fogged up. Probably why he's such a dog's ass outfit."

"Probably."

"Yeah, well he doesn't sound like a man I'd worry too much about if I were you, which I'm not of course. Any story he hands you is probably legit. You still got suspicions, I can hang a loose tail on him."

"What's the fee?"

"C-note an hour."

Fuck me! Who would have the balls to charge one hundred dollars an hour for a tail? I waited a few seconds to make it appear I was thinking it over. Then I said, "No, forget him."

"Okay. Next up, Orlando Finney. Most of what I uncovered on Finney so far is public record. He's been a small-time hood all his adult life. Pimps, pushes dope, recently he thinks his calling in life is fleecing wetbacks from what little money they got. He did a stretch in Vandalia and another one in Joliet."

"I know all that."

"Yeah, well one of my operatives happens to be Mex. You know how Chicago is getting these days; you can't do a lot of business unless you *se habla español*. So I got one. Anyway, this Mex of mine says Finney is well known in the Mex community. My Mex says Finney is a wetback contractor. He's the man to see if you need IA's for a construction job or if you're a farmer needing to get some tomatoes picked. These wetbacks get paid like three bucks an hour to do some ball-busting job you couldn't find no one else to do for ten or twelve. And on top of that, the wets kick back part of that three dollars to Finney." The man started to laugh. "Guess where he works out of?"

"Tell me."

"Maxwell Street." The man found this so funny he sounded like he was doubled over. "Is that a good one? Maxwell Street? Supposedly, and I say supposedly because I haven't found it out yet, there is a phone number you can call during the week if you make it worth Finney's while, but most people show up on weekends at Maxwell Street and hire what they need. They'll have a Hookers To Go operating out of there next."

"Where is he now?"

Like that his voice got serious. "Yeah, I know, that's what you needed most. I don't know I got to tell you honest. So far I got three addresses on him, but he's not at any of them. It's only been a couple of days so ordinarily I wouldn't worry, but if you suspect he's skipping to avoid debts, it could be very difficult to run him down. I can find him if you want. It'll take time and it'll cost."

It was Cantel's money, so I said, "Yeah, do that."

There were more chewing sounds, then the voice said, "Where you going to be, Mr. Cantel? You're never home. I called the Lounge. You weren't there, they said *you* were going to be out of town for a while. I was about to quit on this number. What gives?"

"I'll stay in touch," I said. "Give me the number again."

"Mr. Cantel, you already called me once," the man said, sounding confused.

"I lost it."

He read me a number and I hung up. There was a Chicago Commercial yellow pages book underneath the phone. I leafed to the detectives-private listings. Ran my fingers down the page until I found the number in front of me. The Pat Rick AAA Confidential Agency. I'd heard of the guy. I planned to meet him real soon. Suggest his motto should be We Constantly Sleep. Reading your preliminary report over the telephone to a client you only met once. First class confidential work, Rick, you schmuck.

And not only that, but I got your "slow on the uptake" and "dog's ass" hanging.

TWENTY-NINE

At 5:15, Medina and his map-faced compadre sat across from Elvia and me at the end table in Barkers. I said, "Order what you want. It's Stacey Ford's treat. And while I'm eating, I don't wanna hear one argument out of you two." I pointed at Medina, then Elvia. They sat across from each other.

At six, I was sipping a second black coffee. Medina and his

friend still devoured french fries like they hadn't eaten since Christmas. I got pissed. No one had spoken a word. The only noise was chewing. I said, "To get a fucking conversation going here, I'd like to say that Elvia and I are still hunting for the bag of money her brother stole from her. Can you help us find it?"

Medina looked up, lips glossy with grease, annoyance altering his pudgy face. "No, I can't do that. Besides, the money isn't Elvia's, no matter what she says." He gave her a quick look, but she didn't erupt so he looked back at me. "Some wino crashin' at that hotel has probably been making whoever makes Wild Irish Rose rich with that money."

"You think some stranger blundered onto it?"

He wiped shiny fingers on his green sweatshirt. Said, "I don't know what I think."

"Who was the King who went up the stairs at the Elizabeth Monday morning two hours before I did?"

"No King—"

I cut in. "Medina, a King went up the stairs."

"If it was a King, I don't know what King."

"If it was a King, you would know."

Elvia started to say something. I looked at her and she stopped.

Medina said, "I hear you do a lot of drugs."

"What is going on here? I just talked to a guy a little while ago said the same thing. Somebody stick a full page ad in the *Tribune*? Dan Kruger does drugs. Just about everybody I know does drugs. What's everybody coming down on me for?"

"Hey, man, I don't mean to start you off. It's just that you might be a little more open to what I've got to say. You like cocaine?"

"I live by the Muddy Waters get-high credo. You know what that is?"

He looked at me blankly.

I said, "Bring me champagne when I'm thirsty, bring me reefer when I wanna get high. But sure as Muddy's my name, I don't mess around with no cocaine." I smiled, but Medina just kept staring. He didn't know what the hell I was talking about. I said, "Muddy Waters was a bluesman. Those are the lyrics from a song.

"Oh, yeah. I think I heard of him."

I said, "I can't afford coke anyway. That's why I do pills."

"Yeah, I dig pills too, but I love cocaine. Makes me feel like a genius."

"Then it must be a miracle drug."

He looked around the room, leaned forward, talked softly. "Let me lay the scene for you. We're going to start dealing it. Big time. I got plans for the Romeo Kings. I wanna be the biggest gang in Chicago. Not just the biggest Mexican gang, the biggest period. Bigger'n the Vice Lords, the El Rukns—all those guys. Lots of smaller outfits are tryin' to hook up with us. We got us a connection now who deals direct with Miami. We can flood the West Side and Loop with coke. You know about free base?"

"Just what I read and hear."

"Base is like paradise."

"I hear it's the devil."

"No, man, it is heaven. The greatest high ever. One hit and it explodes inside you. It's like having an orgasm in your brain. And you set up these houses and people bring their pipes and their money and they'll sit there all day, just suckin' on that pipe until—" while searching for the right word, he flung his hands in the air—" forever. Or until their hearts give out. They stay awake for days just suckin' the pipe. Rich dudes go through entire savings accounts in two, three days. It's wild. Smack addicts better start to worry because it's gonna get where nobody's gonna mess with that stuff. Not enough profit. A junkie can only do so much heroin before he nods out or just sits around dreamin'. But free basers." He leaned forward more, resting his elbows on the table. "They don't quit. And the high lasts so short a period of time, they just keep doing it and doing it. I got a friend on the South Side. Colored dude. He's been dealing coke to these LaSalle Street dweebs. The commodity brokers and pit traders. These guys got money out the ass and they are *really* into the pipe. He's been working Rush Street for only six months. Six months. Started out with nothing. One room apartment, one suit, a beat-to-hell Dodge. Today, he's got two Cadillacs he bought cash, wears a full length mink coat, got five diamond rings. He dresses like Billy Dee Williams. Got a bitch looks like Whitney Houston. But thinner 'cause she does the pipe too. He showed me two suitcases full of cash. He's got the suitcases sittin' in his bedroom closet for when he needs walking around money. And you wanna hear the best part?"

"He's the new NBA official coke dealer."

"They gave him a Uzi. A machine gun, man. His coke man in Florida *gave* him a Uzi to keep by the front door so if the narcs rush his house he can mow 'em down like rats."

I said, "That's all way cool if your goal in life is to look like a *GQ* cover and pose like a Rambo poster."

"You know what I mean. I'm talking big money. And it's free. Can you get behind that, Kruger? Free money?"

"Free? If your new connection deals with Miami that means somewhere along the line the real connection is the Jamaican and Venezuelan boys, which means sooner or later *you'll* be in contact with them. And if you come in contact with the Jamaican cocaine boys and make one little mistake, your people will die. And not just the gangbangers and homeboys. Those maniacs kill whole buildings full of people just to make sure they get the sucker who ticked them off. It's the same as swattin' flies to them. They are brutal. If that's your idea of free money—"

Medina's buddy was smirking. He blew a kiss at me.

I said, "But then again, they have never run into the Romeo Kings. The roughest, toughest gang in the whole U.S. of A."

The smirk went away. Rand McNally said, "You bein' smart?"

"Sarcastic, actually. Always select the correct word, son. That way you keep the misunderstandings to a minimum."

"You know, you don't know a thing about me, man. About what I can do."

"I know one thing, you're too stupid to run away from a man with a knife in his hand."

"I don't run away from nothin.'"

"That'll look impressive on your tombstone. 'This moron wouldn't run away from nothin.'"

He lifted his voice at me even more. "Okay, man, that is it." He stood, grabbed the front of my shirt and pulled me toward him. I punched his hand in the air.

Medina said, "Shut *up*, Juan, and sit down." People sitting near us inched their chairs away, but didn't look at us. Medina stared at Juan until he was sure Juan was reasonably docile, then started to talk to me in a patient voice. "Yeah, I heard all about them people. I understand they are vicious and violent. But I plan to not make them mad. To make this kind of money you got to be prepared to take risks. Long as they play fair, I will play fair."

"Fine, that's your business, Enrique. What's our business? Why am I here? Just because I pop a few speeders and tranks doesn't mean I plan to graduate to a cocaine habit. And I sure don't plan to commence dealing the stuff. I do drugs, I don't deal drugs. I don't have any rich friends you can turn into addicts, so I hope none of these reasons is why I'm here."

Medina sat back and crossed his arms over his chest. Said, "Nothing like that. The deal is maybe you *can* work for us."

"I thought Kings took care of their own problems."

"It's not working for us directly. Listen, that money Finney had was for us. It was a payoff—"

Elvia started to talk Spanish again. I said quietly, without looking at her, "Elvia, shut up! You want to argue this, you argue later."

She stopped talking, but her arm quivered against mine and I could almost feel the fury jumping from it.

Medina said, "Somebody hired you to find Finney, right?"

"All I'm trying to find is the money. But Finney is also looking for the money, so we bump into each other on occasion. Now I know for sure you're looking for the money. We should all get together and have a party."

Medina said, "My deal is this. When you find Orlando Finney, call me first. Give me thirty minutes before you call the dude who hired you. That's all you gotta do. You can call the dude who hired you, I don't wanna cheat you out of your fee. Just give me the first call and some time."

"Why can't you find him?"

"We're trying, but it's not so easy for us to go some places in town like it is for you."

"You'll probably find him before me."

"No harm done. When you call me, I'll say thank you very much and send a little something along in appreciation. Either way, it'll be worth your while."

"I can't set people up for murder. Not even Orlando Finney. I got a conscience to worry about. Puts me at a disadvantage with guys like you."

"We're not going to kill him." He did not sound convincing and he wouldn't look me in the face. After some seconds, he said, "Okay, maybe he will die, but, Christ, I told you that was *our* money. It was on its way to us."

"Why?"

"A business deal."

"From who?"

"Why do you worry about stuff like that? Take my word, it's important we find him. Being in the business we are in and planning to expand that business like we are, it's essential that nobody perceives us as—weak or vulnerable."

"You mean if word hits the street that Finney ripped you off big-time and you didn't do anything about it, everybody would give it a try."

"Something like that could happen, yes."

"I admit you'd be doing the city a favor, but I can't cop to it in my head. Besides, I wouldn't know where to start looking for him. There's a PI with more resources than me looking for him and he can't find him either."

"You talked to him this morning."

"He gave my friend a phone number. No doubt a pay phone God knows where. Only thing I can tell you is it sounded like somebody was operating a jackhammer about a foot and a half away from him. So look around construction areas. This isn't a thing you honestly expected me to consider, is it? Because if it is you must be totally out of ideas. Besides, Elvia took the money. She's the one you should be ticked at."

Elvia swung her head to glare at me. I smiled wide in reply.

Medina said, "No, it was Finney's responsibility to deliver that money and keep it safe until he did. And I know she doesn't have it anymore because if she did, she sure wouldn't be hanging out with you."

THIRTY

An hour later, Elvia and I crept south through rush hour traffic on Lake Shore Drive. She was tight lipped and blowing out big sighs of air, letting me know that in her rage she was unable to even breathe normally.

Frankly, I didn't give a damn. I liked Elvia well enough, but now that I knew she had a spoiled child side to her, I felt more like a babysitter than a partner. I realized how bad she wanted—thought she needed—this money, but I don't work well even in great partnerships and this one was starting to fall way short of great.

After twenty minutes, she said, "Where are we going?" Her voice was feather soft and pointedly calm. The tone a talker uses to let the listener know it's taking a superhuman effort to stay in control.

I said, "The Midnight Lounge."

"Why?"

"Have a drink or three, look at tits."

She exhaled noisily again. I said, "Ooh, your blood's boiling."

"Don't make fun of me."

I said, "I can tell you're upset, Elvia. You don't have to breathe like an asthmatic and talk like Norman Bates."

"Back there you embarrassed me in front of those pigs. You reprimanded me in public like I was a child."

"Too bad. I warned you straight off. Every time we talk to somebody, sooner or later you start shouting. Control that temper, Elvia, or one of us is gonna get hurt and I'm afraid it might be me. These aren't Young Republicans we've been huddling with. They're violent and they've got tempers set on *now*. You screaming names at them does not work in our best interest."

"They aren't Superman either. You're so scared of everybody, I don't know how you get any work finished."

"I've done this work for a long time. I know what I'm doing. Sort of. And this is *business*." I sliced my right hand sideways through the air. "That's all it is. Business. I hope we find the money, but we probably won't. If what Medina just told us is true, the money is theirs. If they can't get the money, it looks like Finney's butt will suffice. I know now why Finney is so desperate to find that bag. But if you'll stand back and look at this, you'll see that everybody involved realizes this is *business*. It's not a mission of God type thing to anybody but you. And in the course of *business*, things can happen that scare the hell out of you. That's happening a lot in this case. To a lot of people. And when I get scared, I take precautions."

She was staring out the side window during all this. She muttered, "The hell with all of you."

I said, "You act like God decided to offer Elvia Reyes a chance to live the good life. There are no guarantees like that, sweetheart. What happened was you were at Finney's, you happened to lift a towel and find some money. You had it a couple of hours, lost it, and now somebody else has it. It's not yours by divine right. But anybody disagrees with you about that, you right away start screaming at them. Being as you're the one who started all this, I'm surprised somebody hasn't whaled a tune on your head by now."

"Are you saying when we find the money we're giving it to *them*?"

"No, but I told you at the top of all this that if we learn the money started out honest, we give it up."

She said, "If Finney and the Romeo Kings are involved, that's not something we have to worry about, I don't think."

I laughed. "You're probably right."

I looked at Elvia. She was smiling in spite of herself. She said, "Boy, honest money. With these people involved, that's a dumb idea."

"And don't misunderstand me. If the Kings find Finney on their own and remove him from the material world, I will not toss and turn that night. And should he take a few of them with him—even better. I won't be turning anybody over to the police. I'm not that ethical, which seems to be a well-known fact. All I want is for you to chill out when we talk to these people. Try to look at it as *business*."

"But it *is* my only chance out."

"Maybe, maybe not. But if you get killed, you aren't going to be queen of Tocambaro or anywhere else."

"If I don't find that money, I hope they do kill me. I've had enough of living like this."

"An extremely stupid attitude, but one you're entitled to. However, I'm not ready to die because I can't locate a bag of money I've never seen and didn't even know existed a week ago. And if Ford or Finney or Medina kills you in a fit of anger while I'm standing next to you, that would make me a witness. I doubt very much that those persons would enjoy having a walking, talking witness to a murder they committed. You understand what I'm getting at?"

"I understand."

"Good. Now if we can find out where the money came from and why it was going to the Kings. And what it was for, although that part I can narrow down easy. Either illegals or drugs. And we need to piece Cantel into all this. We do that, we're in business."

"Business, business, business," Elvia said, mocking me. "I thought we just wanted the money."

"We do. Doing these things might help us get it. It also might save our necks."

"I don't see how."

I said, "When you were at Finney's the night you found the bag, did he say anything about it?"

"No."

We were silent for a mile, then I said, "Do you really not care? Would you really rather die if you don't get this money?"

Elvia didn't answer.

THIRTY-ONE

The greedy Gus bartender at the Midnight Lounge looked at me like I was a loan shark collector when Elvia and I sat down at the end of the bar. No girls were on stage, it was too early. The White Sox-Boston game was on the TV above the end of the bar. The few business types getting an early start gave the game casual attention.

I beckoned. The man walked over and I ordered Tequila straight for both of us. I said, "If Cantel was around, that game wouldn't be on, would it?"

The man didn't want me to know it, but he was more than a little nervous. His hands shook ever so slightly as he poured the liquor. With forced casualness, he said, "Sure it would. We always have the Sox on. Cantel likes to cheer for their opponents. Unless of course a Sox fan with a wad of dough is sittin' here. Then you'd think Cantel was born in Bridgeport."

"Guess that's a sight I'll never see."

His grin was pure contempt. "Doubt it," he said.

"But I'm not here to watch a baseball game."

The grin vanished. "No, you want booze. You and the chiquita want Tequilas. The next two are on the house."

"I wouldn't think of not accepting. You heard from Cantel today?"

Wearily, he said, "I told you once before. *He* is *my* boss. He doesn't report to me. You are familiar with the concept? Boss? Worker?"

"Heard anything about where he's hiding out?"

"He ain't hiding out. Why would he have to hide out? He's on a business trip."

"That he decided to take three hours before he left. That he financed with panic money he kept stashed in the office safe."

"Like I said, he don't explain his actions to me. I only work here. Come to think of it, I don't have to explain his actions to you."

"You've talked too much already, better not stop now. He check in with whoever is running the place in his absence? Just to make sure you guys don't turn the place into a gay bar or something?"

"Couldn't say."

"What about the business out of the office? Who runs that when Cantel is out of town?"

He frowned, then moved to the other end of the bar to pump a draft for an arriving silver-haired man in a brown suit. He didn't want to continue our conversation so he stayed at that end, pretending there were water rings to be rubbed away.

He probably didn't have a clue as to what was going on, which can make a man plenty nervous. All he knew for sure was I spelled trouble. One day he's sliding glasses to horny lushes, minding his own business, when out of the blue here I come asking a ton of questions, conning Alice Baker's address out of him, bribing him so I can visit the Boss's office. Next thing he knows, his boss is tossing money into a suitcase, pissed off big time, firing a million questions at him, and lighting out for God knows where. I know from lots of experience what it's like to be completely in the dark and sensing that things are going straight to hell all around you. Makes for some uneasy thoughts. This guy would probably give a year of his life to have those two conversations with me back again. If Cantel ever found out I knew about the murders and then found out I knew because this poor sap of a beer pourer walked me to his office for twenty bucks, there'd be another headline in the *Sun-Times*.

I watched the Sox for a bit. The inning ended and the score flashed on the screen. Red Sox 6, White Sox 0. Only the third. I winced. Another long summer. I motioned to the beer pourer. He walked toward us reluctantly.

I put a ten on the bar. "Beer this time. Dos Equus. Keep the change."

He grimaced like he had stomach flu. Said, "You're too generous, *sir.*"

"Again. Cantel call anybody here today?"

"Again. I don't know."

"Listen, friend, I *need* to know these things. I'm not asking out of idle curiosity. You stiff me and when Cantel finally shows,

I'll tell him how easy it is to find his office."

"I'll explain I thought you were another of his junkie friends. You look the part."

"I doubt very much that's accepted practice, taking strangers to his office when he's not here, but even if it is, it wouldn't get you off the hook this time. Once I started talking, he'd realize the trouble he was in, and he'd know it was all because of you. He'd get upset and when he gets upset—" I let it hang.

The man's face fell like a month-old Jack O'Lantern. He didn't know about the four murders, of course, he didn't know what the hell I was alluding to, but he knew what happened when Cantel got upset. He said, "So what's the deal this time?" He looked at the men sitting to my right, but they were watching the Red Sox tattoo another pathetic White Sox reliever. There was a man two stools down from Elvia. He was watching Elvia. Long, lingering up and down visual caresses. That made the bartender notice her, too. He said, "What about the girl?"

"Can't speak a word of English."

Elvia smiled wide at the bartender, then kicked my ankle, her face never changing.

I'd been looking at her as he and I talked. I smiled at her, teeth held tight together to hold in the pain. I turned back to the man and said, "I need to know the name of the cop who is a very good friend of Cantel's."

"He's got a lot of cop friends. It's good for business."

"This one is more than just friends. He's on the payroll. Italian guy. Big, flat nose, thick lips, forehead looks like someone caved it in with a crowbar."

He screwed his face up like he was trying to remember, but he knew who I meant. I read that in his eyes. They showed a lot of fear.

I said, "Late twenties, early thirties. Talks tough, probably is. But says it so sweetly."

He leaned forward, resting his forearms on the inner part of the bar, put his face near mine. He whispered savagely, "I already put my neck in a noose for you. You think twenty bucks last time and ten now is some kind of fucking fortune? I'm gonna retire on it? You think I wanna lose my job and maybe get my ass kicked for thirty stinking bucks?"

I said, "Your boss is in bigger trouble than you can imagine. No doubt he is in a rage the likes of which even you've never seen. With what I could tell him, not only would you lose your job, you'd end up begging him to only kick your ass." I didn't bother to tell him I'd never be providing this information to Cantel because if I did, I'd be dead meat in an eyeblink, shortly before or after him. I went on, "Your best chance to stay solid with your boss is to tell me what I need to know. That will make me happy and keep me from talking to him."

He didn't move his head, which was still inches from mine. He whispered fast and hard, "You're damn right that guy is tough. His name is Nicholas Toreldo. He's a vice cop. Always visits Cantel's office after hours. Delivers for him. He's Narcotics Division. When he's overly juiced, he tells stories I hesitate to repeat."

At first, I didn't believe him. Why would a narc be in a uniform? But then it flashed on me. The uniform was to impress me and confuse me when I attempted to find out who he was. Dirty the waters a bit. I said, "But I love stories."

"Then maybe you'd love to hear what he does to loud mouths who snitch on their friends."

"Not really, but I'd like to know how much he gets on the take."

"He claims three grand a week. Sometimes more, sometimes less."

I whistled. "Cantel pay him?"

"Used to. I don't think so anymore. They got close."

"Toreldo do drugs or just deal?"

"He does 'em."

"Heroin."

"A little. His main passion is coke. I've seen him do amounts of cola that'd kill you or me. Guy's a complete addict. He brings in the coke he scores in busts. He turns some in, keeps the rest for himself. He brags he could develop a grand a day habit and never have to pay a penny. He knows who to shake down."

"When was he in here last?"

"Early this morning."

"Looking for Cantel?"

"Yeah. I told him Cantel had beat it. Didn't know why."

"Tell him about the suitcase?"

"Yeah."

"He didn't say nothin'?"

"Nope. Just said okay."

And not too long after that, he'd delivered Cantel's message to me. So somebody knew how to get in touch with Iron Jaw Cantelli.

THIRTY-TWO

Walking across Wabash to the Pago Pago lot, Elvia asked, "What was that remark about 'no English' supposed to mean?"

"Just a joke."

"I didn't think it was funny."

"Then I'm sorry."

"It was condescending. You've treated me like a child all day."

"Quit pouting and I'll stop."

"I get scolded and barked at in front of trash like the Kings and now I'm treated like an ignorant Mex in front of a bartender in a sleazy lechers joint. You treat me like this because I'm a woman or Mexican?"

"Neither. I said it was supposed to be a joke."

"Stop humoring me and start treating me like a partner, not a child or a joke."

I stopped walking. So did she. I said, "This partnership is not exactly a symphony, know what I mean? I'm sick of the bickering. Back there was said as a joke. I understand why you didn't think it was funny and I said I was sorry. So drop it." I started walking again.

She fell in step. "Well, you complain when you're upset with me."

"I realize that. It's okay. It was a dumb thing to say; I don't always think before I speak. But maybe he wouldn't've told us

Toreldo's name if he thought you understood English."

"Don't try to wiggle out of it."

I smiled. "You have to admit he was *very* scared of Toreldo and he probably wouldn't want a lot of people knowing he supplied me the name."

Elvia said, "What was all that stuff you were holding over that man's head about Cantel? You suggested you knew something that would get him put away for a long time."

"That, partner, is something I don't tell you or anybody else."

"Dan—"

"No negotiations. I often get the impression you haven't been entirely honest with me. You've got some secrets you're hiding, right?"

"Of course not."

"Liar. You got secrets and that one is my secret."

We drove to Halsted, turned north. It was early dusk and the Loop was still emptying. Traffic surged forward in tiny increments, horn yelps ricocheted off the skyscraper canyons and the El. I asked Elvia if she could handle another visit to apartment 519.

She said, "I can handle it but you were just there this morning. Why do we have to go back?"

"I need to know more about Toreldo. Everything I've seen and heard about the man spells big time trouble."

"What would Ford know about him?"

"Maybe nothing, but Ford's in this mess a lot deeper than he planned to go, I think. He's the one person who seems to be familiar with everybody else. He might know something about Toreldo and be willing to tell it now that he's nervous and broke. I'm sure he ran back to Vicki's apartment because he's got no place else to go. How much of his money is left?"

"Two hundred. About."

"Keep fifty. We'll offer him a hundred fifty if it appears he knows something and feels like talking about it. That's fifty percent of his original roll. Hand it over."

"I don't think this is wise."

"I'm sure you don't. But I guarantee he won't talk to us for free. Not after this morning. The chance of making a deal to get back half his wad might loosen his tongue a little. Least he could scram town with a hundred fifty."

She made a pained face, but lifted her butt off the seat and took the money from the back pocket of her jeans. She straightened the folded in third roll, slid off two twenties and a ten and pushed them down the front of her pants, handed me the rest, which I put in my jacket pocket next to the pill bottles.

I said, "You can put that fifty back where you got it. I'm not going to pick your pocket when your back is turned."

She combed her fingers through her blonde-black hair. Looking straight ahead she said, "I don't think I trust any of you people anymore. In my mind I had the good people and the bad people separated. I'm not sure now there is such a separation."

I said, "Welcome to the real world, Elvia. Personally, I blame society for making me the amoral creature I am today. But just because I treat my partner like a child when my brain's in reverse doesn't mean I'd steal their money. Besides, you're a fine one to talk. You stealing the money is what set all this going."

"Don't start."

I chuckled.

It took us another forty-five minutes to find a parking spot, and walk to Fairview Gardens.

The door of 519 was open slightly. I hadn't expected that. In this neighborhood it screamed trouble. I told Elvia to wait in the hallway.

I called Vicki's name softly, then Stacey's, through the gap between the door and the jamb. There was no answer. I pushed the door open more and stepped inside. It was too dark to see. I flipped the switch by the door and an overhead hallway light blinked on.

I saw Vicki right away. She was on the floor, fifteen feet from me, face down. Her legs were in the hallway; her torso in the living room, raised slightly by a half-step in the doorway that led into that room from the hall. I moved closer to see all of her. Her arms flopped out from her body. I figured she had turned and tried to run away from the killer at the front door. She hadn't got far when a large caliber bullet exploded the back of her head. She was wearing a cocktail waitress type outfit, white blouse, short red skirt, black hose. Except now the upper back of the blouse was as red as the skirt. There was an oblong shaped puddle of blood leaking from under her face, probably from her nose, which no doubt smashed flat when she landed. Coming from the face the puddle looked like a red paragraph bar drawn from the mouth of a character in a comic strip.

I whispered back to Elvia, "Don't come in here."

"Are they dead?"

"The woman is."

Then she was next to me, looking down at Vicki. She said, "Where's Ford? Did he kill her?" She didn't sound at all upset or scared. Just curious.

"I don't think so."

"Who did?"

"Offhand I couldn't narrow it any lower than ten or twelve people. You can only play so many punks against each other for so long. How many other rooms in the apartment?"

Elvia seemed entranced by the body. Not taking her eyes off it she said, "The kitchen's on the right, the bedroom and bathroom on the left down the hall." She pointed.

I went beyond the sparse light the overhead bulb gave off into the dark interior. I turned on lights in the kitchen and bathroom but there was nothing in those rooms. When I got to the bedroom, I pretty much knew what I was going to find. I squinched my eyes, turned on the light.

After some seconds, I opened them. Stacey Ford was lying on the yellow carpeted floor just to the left of a double bed with a cream quilt. His feet pointed at me as I stood in the doorway. The back of his head was a pulpy, matted mess. So was the carpet. He wore jeans and a white T-shirt, his feet were bare. From the placement of his body, I suspected that wherever he'd been in the apartment when he heard the shot that killed Vicki, he'd scrambled down the hallway and into the bedroom, intending to burrow under the bed. A pathetic attempt at flight and concealment, but it's an ingrained response in all of us and this was the only chance he had. There was only one way out and the killer was between Ford and it.

On the nightstand next to the bed was the well-thumbed copy of *The Grapes of Wrath* he'd had in the glove compartment when we went to see Joseph Cantel. I walked over and picked it up, careful not to step in the blood. Page 24 still had a dog-ear mark and I wondered how many more times he'd reread the first 23 pages. Next to the book was a sandwich bag. Inside the bag, a pencil-wide line of white powder was caked along the bottom crease. I touched the powder with my index finger, brought it up and rubbed it against my gums below my bicuspids. Coke. Stacey and Vicki were feeling fine up to the time she'd answered the door.

Elvia walked into the bedroom. She looked down at Ford. A small smile crossed her face, was gone so quickly I might've imagined it. Then she said, "Son-of-a-bitch," and spat on his back. She kicked his ribs like a placekicker attempting a fifty yard field goal.

I said, "Don't leave an impression of your shoe in the blood, Elvia." I figured it was healthy and necessary for her to outlet some of her rage and frustration by kicking the shit out of the corpse of the man who'd raped her twice. Anyway, Ford wasn't objecting.

But I couldn't watch so I opened dresser drawers and looked in the closet, sliding slacks and dresses around. There was nothing of interest. I hadn't expected there would be. Vicki was just a friend of Stacey Ford who liked him enough or felt sorry enough to let him crash at her place when he had nowhere else to go. I felt a wave of pity for Vicki. Another desperately lonely person not getting any younger who couldn't pick friends worth a damn, or worse, had to settle for whatever friends picked her. Either way, she didn't deserve to die.

Behind me, Elvia was muttering in Spanish and I heard hollow thunks and cracks from more kicks. Then the words and the thunks stopped and I turned to look at her. She leaned against the doorway, hands in pockets, watching me stand in the middle of the room, looking around, wondering if there was anything else I should check for before we left.

She said, "There was twenty dollars on the kitchen table. I took it."

"Good. If you didn't the cops would."

"And give me back the hundred fifty."

I did. Said, "Let's get out of here."

THIRTY-THREE

Back in the Skylark, I told Elvia that was it—I was through for the day. I waited for the explosion and accusations of cowardice, but she just said, "Okay," distractedly. Two corpses caused even Elvia Reyes to pause and reflect.

Halfway to the hotel she asked, "You positive you don't know who killed them?"

I said, "No," but I was lying. Joseph Cantel believed there was only one person who could link him to the four murders; the man who introduced those men to him—Staccy Ford. Plus Ford had dropped me in Cantel's lap and Cantel didn't have the foggiest idea why. Ford was freaking Cantel out. On Roosevelt Road, I witnessed how Cantel operated when he thought he was being set up, but I doubted Cantel was still in Chicago. That left one person—Nick Toreldo. No doubt Cantel had explained the entire predicament to Toreldo. Cantel didn't know I'd seen him at Curtis Hopkins' apartment, so Toreldo was supposed to only scare me away. But Ford could put two and two together so he had to die. Being a cop, Toreldo could check out the whereabouts of Stacey Ford by calling station houses. Ford was the type of punk the police keep half an eye on. At some house, some cop said, "Oh yeah, Stacey Ford, hillbilly druggie, we got him staying with his floozy, Vicki whatever, at Fairview Gardens, apartment 519." And that was it for Stacey Ford. No wonder he was so scared in front of my apartment. He knew how this crowd operated. I was still learning.

And what I was learning made me sick. I wished with all my heart I'd never talked to May Carter.

My thoughts were getting increasingly negative and extremely depressing so I stopped at a package liquor store. Bought two large bottles of brandy. In the car, I drank a long slug, then swallowed a Valium. Immediately felt the friendly fire kindle in my belly. I handed the bottle to Elvia. She sipped greedily. She realized Ford and Vicki's death meant nothing good for us, even if she didn't know why exactly. The vibes I was giving off must've influenced her in some way. Fear is as contagious as influenza.

The May thing would not leave my mind. We were only two blocks from the hotel when I decided I had to check on her. I swung the Skylark right, went a block, turned right again. Headed south.

Elvia said, "Now what?"

"I got to get May out of that apartment."

"I thought you said she had another day or two."

"That was then."

"Dan, when are you going to tell me what's going on?" Her voice contained more than a pinch of panic.

I didn't answer.

I didn't know if Toreldo would ever show at Alice Baker's apartment. I couldn't think of what the reason would be, but if he did and May happened to be there, of course he'd ask what the hell was going on. Why was a colored junkie crashing in Joseph Cantel's girlfriend's apartment? May, being your typical junkie scared to death of any cop because a cop can lock a junkie up where a junkie can't get any junk, would tell the whole story, hoping with typical junkie logic, that the cop would say, "Oh sure, it's okay if *Dan Kruger* told you you could stay here so you could hide from Joseph Cantel because you know Cantel killed your boyfriend"—I didn't think about it anymore.

Soon the Vitamin V kicked in and I was able to detach a bit. Face my fate with a shred of serenity, however artificial. The comforting thought came to me that at least Toreldo dispatched his victims quickly.

Three blocks north of Alice Baker's apartment, I saw a walking example of the famous Dan Kruger luck. Dan Kruger luck floats above my head like a sadistic vulture, constantly ready to divebomb when it gets the chance.

Of course Nick Toreldo had checked out Alice Baker's apartment. She'd probably forgotten her favorite earring and Cantel asked Toreldo to kindly fetch it. And of course May was there. Higher than the moon.

They were walking side by side up Wabash, under the sloppy orange glare of the sodium streetlights. He wore an open trenchcoat over a brown suit and walked briskly, face in a frown. His right hand was on the small of her back, keeping her in step. May's arms were wrapped across her chest, her face impassive. She had sunglasses on and wore a long sleeve black shirt and no jacket. No doubt strung out on the last score of heroin she'd ever need. One last ride on the white horse.

I muttered, "Dammit!" They passed even with us and I shifted the mirror to follow them down the street. Toreldo was parked half a block behind us. He opened his passenger door, shoved May inside, then slammed the door shut and hurried around the back of the car to his side.

I looked over at Elvia. She had a puzzled expression on her face. She must not have seen them, she didn't say anything.

I said, "Elvia, for your own sake, you better scare up a new partner. As of now your current one's future prospects are nil."

THIRTY-FOUR

We traded sips of brandy all the way back to the hotel. The brandy sat on top of the Valium and I didn't feel near as panicky as I should have. At some point in the drive, Elvia had said, as though she'd been thinking it over carefully, "We're still partners." I shrugged in reply.

The tile stairs were as sticky as the floor of the Oriental Theater at midnight. At the top of the fifth flight, we turned left to get to our room. As we did, I saw a man and a woman headed toward us down the hallway. I shied backwards around the corner, pushing Elvia behind me. I stepped down to the top step, put my arm across her. The couple got to the stairs and I relaxed. A middle-aged Oriental woman with her upper two front teeth missing and black hair hanging to her waist was pushing away a tall hillbilly-looking kid who grinned like Goofy and kept trying to wrap his arm around her shoulder.

They started down the stairs, not paying us any attention.

They smelled like Thunderbird was their cologne of choice.

"You lied to me," the woman said. She spat in the kid's face.

"I never lied to you," the kid said, lamely, wiping the spit away with his sleeve. "My friends lied to you."

They continued down the stairs, the sound of their conversation becoming faint as they got a floor below us.

I looked at Elvia. We both tried to grin. I said, "Life's a bitch all over."

We sat on the edge of our beds, facing each other, traded more sips of brandy. Bugs, free from the cage, scampered around the room. I watched him, became briefly maudlin, wondering who would take care of the little guy if Toreldo nailed my butt. Then I told myself he didn't have me yet. That was the important thing. I was still alive. And I was a seasoned, reasonably intelligent PI. Old DK had been around a bit. Fucking A. I knew a little about survival. I was no May Carter. He'd have to catch me unaware, Jack. Like when I was drunk as hell. And fat chance of that happening more than two or three times a day.

At 10:00, Elvia lay down "to rest" and next thing she was snoring like a prizefighter. Clothes on, curled in a ball, on top of the blankets. I untied and removed her shoes, worked the blankets down under her, pulled them up over her. I kicked my shoes off, lay down on the other bed. Closed my eyes. Immediately a thousand thoughts zoomed forward, each one demanding immediate attention. Sometimes I *know* when it's hopeless to try for sleep. Tonight was one of those sometimes.

So I got up and slid the SG case from under the bed. I unsnapped it and removed the guitar. I tiptoed to the door, pulled it open and, sticking just my head out, cased up and down the hall. It was deserted. I slipped out and sat down cross-legged, back against the wall. I left the door open a little in case I needed to scoot inside. I set the brandy bottle next to me. Not much left now. But the second one sat unopened on the nightstand inside so I wasn't concerned.

I started squeezing off blues riffs. Eight and ten note flurries, then long, keening bends. I played in A, making the four and five chords, D7 and E7, once in a while for reference, but mostly just playing licks. After each verse I sipped brandy. Maybe that was why I started sounding like Buddy Guy. Damn, I could *play*! Why hadn't I pursued this instead of a dead end career like private investigation? Ten more minutes passed and I was ready for a man to man smokeout with Otis Rush. Bugs stuck his nose out the door, hopped through. He lay down next to me, rolled on his back, paws in the air, trancelike from the beauty and fire of my playing.

I was so caught up in my groove that I never heard the man approach, and when the voice spoke above my head, I almost had the massive coronary I fully expect will carry me off this planet someday soon. It scared Bugs too. He flipped right side up and streaked into the room.

I looked up at an elderly black man with a heavy stubble of white beard wearing striped green pants, an electric blue shirt and a jaunty Tyrolean hat. He said, "Well, how come?"

I said, "How come what?" My scared heart chugged like a locomotive.

The man had a bottle in his hand. Wild Irish Rose. The quintessential wino's wine. He offered it to me. I took a sip. I handed him the brandy bottle. He killed it, then said, "How come all you white boys who play guitar are all the time playin' like old black men? This is something that have been bothering me for a long time. Only black people I know who listen to the blues anymore live in Mississippi or are like 95 years old, but you white boys be playin' it all over the damn place."

"How's it sound?"

He laughed and swayed like a cobra readying to bite. "Well, drunk as I am at this time, it don't sound half bad, but damn, I mean all you white boys want to do is play the blues. Fast, slow or whatever. I just want to know how come?"

I said, "It beats hell out of Lawrence Welk." I played another riff, gave the strings extra bending now that I had an audience. Stopped suddenly, said, "But maybe over at Cabrini Green, right now even as we speak, there's a bunch of young brothers listening to old Perry Como and Eddie Fisher records. And they're buying cashmere sweaters and gray hush puppies at secondhand shops and they're sitting on those like tall bar stools, snapping their fingers and singing "Oh, My Papa" and "Don't Let the Stars Get in Your Eyes". And they're totally blowing off rhythm and are digging on the melody—"

The man was roaring. He said, "Okay, okay. I can *see* it." He stumbled toward the stairway, pitching back and forth, bumping off the wall, laughing his damn head off.

I put my head against the wall. Suddenly, the brandy had zapped my brain and I felt exhausted. Maybe I'd sleep tonight after all.

A minute later, Elvia screamed. I scrambled through the door, slamming it behind me. I held the guitar at the end of the neck, cocked it over my shoulder like it was a baseball bat.

But it was a nightmare that had hold of her, not anything or anybody I could bash into pulp. Her arms thrashed on the mattress like dying fishes and under the sheet her legs tried to kick themselves free. She shouted things in Spanish, then screamed again as I moved fast to the bed. I sat on the edge of it, shook her hard.

It took some seconds for her to come up from under the dream. When her eyes opened, she blinked twice, then recognition came. She sat up, wrapped her arms around my neck and pulled me down with her. She whispered quickly, "Dan, I am so scared right now. Stay here tonight. With me. Please?"

I whispered that I would.

Later, we were still naked, but our breathing was back to normal, and we lay there, her leg hitched over my hip, our stomachs sweat-suctioned together.

I asked what the dream had been.

She said, "Somebody killed you and they were coming after me."

"Where was this?"

"I'm not sure. It was a big place. Lots of rooms, all of them connected together. Some of them looked like this room, some were like the bedroom at the Fairview Gardens apartment. It changed back and forth from room to room. And everything was dark. It was night and there wasn't any lights on in any of the rooms, but I could tell what each room looked like. They were lit with moonlight."

"Who chased you?"

"I don't know. I'd run into a room and whoever it was would kick the door down behind me. But there was always a second door for me to escape through and I'd slam it behind me and they'd kick *that* one down."

"How'd you know I was dead?"

"I fell over you. That was just before you woke me up. You were lying in that bedroom at the Fairview Gardens next to the bed just like Stacey Ford. Face down, head exploded, everything the same. What made everything even more scary was the silence. It was dead silent. I wasn't even screaming until I saw you; the person chasing me wasn't saying anything. There wasn't even any sound when they crashed through the doors. But I kept hearing something outside. Like a wailing or shrieking. I ran to a window, which suddenly appeared, and saw my mother walking up and down the street in front of this hotel. There weren't any cars or other people or anything else out there. Just her standing under a streetlamp. She was dressed old-fashioned, like grandmothers dress in Mexico, and she was screaming, but not like a human being would scream. It was abnormal, like a monster in a horror movie. She kept yelling her baby was dead." Elvia shuddered and I held her tighter. After a bit, she said, "We're in a lot of trouble, aren't we? I can tell by the way you've been acting tonight."

"I don't know about us. I am."

"Then we both are. Are we going to find the money?"

"I really doubt it, Elvia. I always have."

"I think it's still out there. We could still find it. You could come back to Tocambaro with me."

"Be the king of Tocambaro?" I smiled. "I've never been optimistic about finding it, Elvia. You know that."

"So why'd you agree to help me?"

"There was a chance. Then I got drawn into it for other reasons."

"But look what it got you into."

"Just now or the last few days?"

She punched my arm lightly. "I mean the trouble."

"I'm used to trouble. I never like it, but I'm used to it." I paused, then said, "It's greed. Everytime I succumb to it, I pay a price."

"What are we going to do?"

"Try to stay alive."

"How are we going to do that?"

I was thinking 'beats the hell out of me', but I said, "I've got a vague plan, but I wanna sleep on it before I decide if it'll work."

She was silent for a while and I thought she was asleep, then she said, "Dan, are we going to be okay? I mean, really."

I said, "Sure."

At least until tomorrow.

THIRTY-FIVE

Early the next morning, as dawn started to gray the room, we made love again. Gently and slowly. Like we had all the time in the world, which of course we didn't. But it seemed nice to pretend. When we were spent, it was still too early to face whatever was ahead. I asked her, "Are you really going back to Tocambaro if we find this money?"

"Yep." She paused. "Why, don't you want me to leave?"

"I'm used to being left. But I have to say I like you better like this than when we're arguing."

"I like this more, too."

"What's in Tocambaro?"

"My family. Some of them, I think. And a lot of people I'm going to treat like shit."

"Why?"

"That's the way they treated me when I was young."

"Why'd they do that?"

"We were poorer than they were."

"They weren't poor?"

"Sure they were poor, but not as much as us."

"Things were that bad?"

She didn't answer right away. Then she said, "Yep."

"Who are these people?"

"Just people. If they lived here they'd be worse off than junkies or hobos, or—anybody. You'll never understand. You told me how you have no money, you are in the poverty zone. It makes me laugh. Makes me realize you will never understand me, which is why I got so angry. I apologize now. It's not your fault. You just don't *know.*"

"It's okay."

She went on, "You could buy and sell these people I talk about. But they had a few possessions. Like maybe a radio, a black and white TV, two pairs of blue jeans and two American T-shirts. Shoes. And my family had nothing. Except a lot of children and some chickens."

"How many children."

"I don't know for sure. There were seven or eight of us when I was growing up, but I'm sure there were more before us who left when they got to be fifteen or so. My mother wouldn't talk about it so that's why I don't know. They had to leave or the young ones would've been hungry all the time. That's why I left when I did."

"You don't know all your own family?"

"Not really. I knew them, they were always around, but—I was close to one sister, Rosalita. She was the only close friend I had when I was growing up. She was one year older than me. She died."

"When?"

"Just before I left, she got sick." Elvia was quiet again for a while. "She got very sick. There wasn't a doctor close by, even if we could have paid for one. Which we couldn't."

"What disease did she have?"

"I don't know. She threw up blood, she lost all her weight and in a couple of weeks she died."

"Your mother and father still there?"

"I think so. Ricardo said he had seen them two years ago. There were still four young ones there then."

"How old is your mother?"

"I'm not sure. Old though. Too old to have four young children. But maybe they were grandchildren from one of my sisters. Ricardo would never think to ask questions like that."

"Tell me what you're gonna do when you go back."

"With that money I will see to it that my mother and father live like human beings for their last days at least. If they're still alive. And I have a bigger reason. My mother always said none of our family would ever amount to anything. We were cursed she said. She was a devout but very bitter woman. I'm going down there, spend some of that money and say, 'See there, old woman.'"

I would've before, but now I didn't point out that getting rich by stealing someone else's money didn't constitute making it in the conventional sense. To Elvia and her mother, it would mean she had done fine.

I said, "Under the circumstances who could blame her?"

"I know, I know. She was mad about many things. When you've raised that many children and the only hope you see for them to break out of such a miserable life is to be a wetback. Can you imagine? Here, mothers dream of their sons and daughters becoming doctors or lawyers or secretaries. That means they've succeeded. For my mother, success meant crossing a dirty filthy river without getting caught and sent back home."

"Then you succeeded in her eyes."

"But not in mine. My mother saw some of her children die and the rest ended up like my father. All he wanted to do was stay drunk on Tequila and beer."

"What did your father do when he wasn't drunk?"

"Field work mostly. Hired hand. Pick up after festivals. He tried to grow corn and beans, but the land we had was like ashes. And it rains maybe twice a year. Worthless land. That was the only reason he could keep it I suppose. If it had been worth anything my father wouldn't have had it, I guarantee you." She stopped talking and kissed me, laughing a little. Said, "You don't understand, do you?"

She sounded embarrassed.

"I'm starting to. It's difficult to understand why people get totally obsessed with something, but that's only because you've never experienced what they did."

She said, "Does 5,000 pesos sound like a lot of money?"

"I don't know from pesos, but 5,000 anything sounds like a lot."

"It's two dollars, about. That's what my father made a day. On a good day. He worked at this big farm on the other side of the village. Well, not very big compared to farms here, but big for there."

"Two dollars a day with seven or eight kids?"

"Yep."

"You *will* live like a queen with a bag of money down there."

"I won't stay long. Just long enough to set my parents up and just long enough to treat a lot of people like shit. The people who laughed at Rosalita and me because we had one dress to wear, that twenty people had worn already, and no shoes, and never had a bath or anything to put in our hair and were hungry all the time and slept on the floor." She stopped, nestled closer to me, wrapped her arms around me, hugged hard. But she didn't cry because Elvia had stopped crying about the rotten hand she'd been dealt a long time ago. She aimed to avenge it now.

We both nodded off. When I awoke, it was light. Elvia sat naked on the floor on the far side of the room, cross-legged, watching me. She'd showered and was pulling her fingers through her wet hair, letting drops drip onto her shoulders, where they slid down her arms into her lap. She was petting Bugs with her free hand. When she saw I was awake, she said, "I hope I didn't embarrass you about what I talked about before."

"Why would it embarrass me?" But I felt guilty saying it, because it had a little.

"Americans get embarrassed about people as poor as I was. Like we're subhuman to live like that. They think people choose to live like that I guess."

"Don't worry about it."

"So what's this plan of yours?"

"Nothing I'm proud of."

"We don't have too many choices, do we?"

"No we don't."

"So?"

"This morning we visit Maxwell Street. Then we take it from there. First I need breakfast." The second brandy bottle was still on the nightstand. I unscrewed the top, took a generous swig. I shook some white cross from the bottle in my pants. Swallowed them with a second gulp of The Christian Brothers. I screwed the top back on, lay back.

The whole time Elvia watched me, head slanted, still comb-
ing. When I was done, she said, "You do too many drugs and you
drink too much."

"I told you I blame society. And my environment."

"You should stay alert all the time if we're in trouble."

"Alcohol and drugs solve all my problems. Except the biggest
problem I got."

"What's that?"

"Alcohol and drugs." I laughed, she didn't. I didn't blame her.
It's an old joke and I guess not all that funny.

THIRTY–SIX

I wedged the Skylark into a spot in the corner of a lot almost
under the Dan Ryan Expressway on 15th, a few blocks south of
Maxwell Street. As I locked the door, Elvia asked me over the
top of the car, "You buy stuff down here?"

"Just blues tapes. It's not like they hand out warranties with
the rest of the stuff."

We started walking. She said, "I worked a table here the first
year I was in Chicago."

"What'd you hawk?"

"You'll laugh."

"So?"

"Paintings on black velvet."

She was right, I laughed.

"Cliché, right?"

"Every culture has their eccentricities. Polka, voodoo, knee
dancing, square dancing, paintings on black velvet. All the
same."

Maxwell Street takes up a lot more area than just that street.
It's huge. The first thing you notice as you get close to the mar-
ket is the smoke from the scores of grills top heavy with sizzling
Polish sausage and onions, red hots and ribs. It blankets the

entire market area like an August haze. The smell of the meat wafts through the air, overpowering the usual smells of garbage and sweat and poverty.

Throngs of burbies and suckers and maybe even a crafty shopper or two walked with us. In some places it's chic to say "I got it on Maxwell". But what you usually get on Maxwell is took. The vendors—aggressive, haggling types who thrive in open air bazaars—waited for us, licking their lips and fingering their moneyrolls. After a long cold winter they were anxious to re-load. They stood behind or in front of piles of cheap sunglasses, car parts, radios, boom boxes, toys, clothes, furniture, microwave ovens—you name it. You can get anything on Maxwell Street. Including wetbacks.

As the crowds got thicker, Elvia took my hand. She said, "Why are we here?"

I said, "Wait."

Music boomed from ghetto blasters, a different beat every few feet. Hip hop, disco, salsa, funk, blues, calypso, hillbilly. I pointed at a box turned to ten, 1960's James Brown blasting a distorted sound from fried speakers. "This is why I come here."

"The music?"

"And the atmosphere. But definately not the sales."

"You really love music, but you never listen to the radio."

"What's on the radio isn't music." We walked some more. I said, "At Christmas time this old black guy parks the blues bus over there on Halsted in that parking lot." I pointed south of where we were. "It's a old school bus he spray painted bright blue."

Along the side of it, he sets up racks and racks of blues cassettes, and inside the bus, he's got tons of albums. He's got a killer sound system on that bus. So you stand there trying to decide how many tapes you can afford and you got Howling Wolf growling in your ear at meltdown volume about how evil he is and how lowdown his women are. And I mean the bus has got everything you can think of. Bessie Smith, down-home country stuff, Chicago blues, Texas, the greats, guys you never heard of—the works. It's heaven hanging out at that bus at Christmas time."

Elvia was looking up at me, a bemused expression on her

face. She didn't know from blues, Howling Wolf, or the blues bus and she didn't care to learn. I smiled, said, "I'll shut up. It's the speed. Turns me into a motormouth."

The first card table in the first row we came to was piled with rusted pieces of metal that didn't look like anything describable and for sure didn't resemble anything a sane person would part money with to lug home. The next table had a collection of fishing lures. Two old black men stood behind it. Judging from the way the men laughed as they passed a shorty of Old Grandad back and forth, selling the lures was not a major priority for them. There were more tables with more piles of junk. At the end of this row, a Korean family was aggressively trying to unload cheap wallets and purses. "Twenny bucks inna stores. A buck anna half here takes it home."

We turned right. Somewhere ahead a live band was playing blues. I had to check it out. We walked along a lane of tables full of fifth-hand clothes, turned left. There was a small grassy section behind a table loaded with cajun and soul food herbs. Behind the swatch of grass was a wooden fence. The amps were set up in front of the fence. A crowd of maybe thirty people watched and swayed. The band was four black men who could have been anywhere from 60 to 600. A drummer whose kit was a bass drum, snare, and high-hat cymbal, a bass player, a harmonica man, and a singer who was drunk on his ass and wasn't singing anything. He mumbled into the microphone and staggered in little circles, holding the mike stand like it was a dancing partner. There was also a fat, bald white boy with a wispy goatee playing lead guitar on a white Fender Telecaster. Execrably. Out of tune, out of key, out of time, out of clues.

A black man about thirty-five sat on a folding metal chair off to the side of the band. He was hunched over, elbows on knees, staring daggers at the white boy and mumbling to himself. He looked like he hurt.

The speed made my fingers itch. I went to the black man on the folding chair, said, "That's a fine guitar, but that boy is lame."

The man didn't take his eyes off the fat boy. He said, "It's my instrument. It won't never forgive me for this. That is some *shit* pickin'. The motherfucker told me he could play."

"How about I jump in there?"

"You play better?"

"In my sleep."

"Then do it, man. If I take my axe right back after this moth- erfucker she'll freeze up on me. I won't be able to play a note."

It sounds silly, but I knew what he meant. When somebody picks up the SG and makes it sound like a duck getting stepped on, I'm always afraid the guitar will take it personally and con- sider getting even for the embarrassment by making me sound like I got two fingers. But I have never actually told that to any- one, so I figured this dude was a little weirder than me, which is always comforting. I said, "I'll square it for you."

I walked in front of the guitar player. He rolled his head around like Ray Charles; a study in ecstasy as he pushed and pulled strings every which way with no idea of what he was doing, but enjoying the hell out of it none the less. I made a cut signal. The band rushed to a close.

Fat boy handed me the Tele and I put the strap over my shoulder. Did a quick retune. While I did, the boy waddled to a group of friends. They laughed and shook his hand, pounded his back. Either they actually thought he could play or it had been a bet.

The harp player was studying me. I winked, said, "What was that?"

"Started off as 'Born in Chicago.' Didn't end that way. You any better?"

"Richard Nixon could get down better than that clown. 'Mel- low Down Easy'?"

'Mellow Down Easy' is a Little Walter tune from the '50s. The golden age of Chicago blues. A shuffle that every band in Chicago, blues or rock, performs at one time or another. It's a harmonica song so at least I'd have the harp man on my side. He said, "In C."

It sounded great. The band was good. I was nervous from the speed and from the crowd, but it was a good nervous. The kind that scares you into concentrating on your playing so you don't sound like the idiot before me.

When we finished, the crowd was bigger. I asked the guitar player if I could sit in for one more. He nodded, smiling I was happy to see. I turned to the harmonica man, said, "Down in the Bottom." You cannot go wrong with the Wolf in Chicago. It was even better than the first tune. At the end of the last verse, the band vamped, letting me stretch out and show off. I played the same riffs that sounded so tight the night before in the hotel hallway. They sounded sloppier here because I was still nervous a little, but it wasn't bad for a white boy. Especially a white boy who hadn't played in a band for years.

When we finished, I handed the guitar man the Tele. He was appreciative. Said, "I owe you, my man. We are the Stony Island Hawks and we jam here every Saturday and Sunday, April to October. And check out the club listings in the *Sun–Times*. We play the North Side during the week. Bring your own axe sometime. You got a lifetime invite to sit in."

I grinned like a pothead.

He closed his eyes, bent over and did a quick intro with a jazzy feel. The Hawks kicked into a modern type blues thing. Lots of minor and extended chords and a ton more changes than the usual I-IV-V. He was real good. The Tele wasn't mad at him, thanks to me. We stayed for two songs and when we left I gave him the OK sign. He smiled and ripped off a million note riff that was so good it made me laugh.

Elvia was suitably impressed. That's why I started playing in the first place; to impress chicks. She said, "You should play for money."

"I did once. It's rarely fun like that, although that's how you remember it twenty years later. It's more like being broke and crashed out in the back of a van in the middle of nowhere at 3:00 A.M., forcing down a greaseburger and trying to find a cheap hotel." I laughed. "Kind of like being a PI."

I took Elvia's hand and we were back in the crowds. Life had been a series of short, pleasant interludes since I crawled under the covers with her the night before. But that was about to end.

Elvia said, "I'm still not sure why we're here."

"I'm not sure either."

I knew we wouldn't be hearing a vendor shout, "Get your IA's here, folks, lots of illegal aliens." And there wouldn't be a table with wetbacks sitting on it, price tags on lapels, waiting for employers to show. I said to Elvia, "Ask some Hispanics walking around how do we get some illegals. Tell them we got a farm and we need five for the weekend."

"Okay, I realize we are looking for Finney now, but why?"

"Just do it. I want to see where they send us."

The first four men she asked did a lot of edging away and head shaking and hand waving. Spouted torrents of Spanish, but gave us no information. She said all of them denied being IA's, which wasn't what it was all about of course, but with me standing next to her, it was an understandable reaction. *Mojado's* must be careful around gringos asking questions.

So I wised up. Told her to use a sawbuck to fan herself with the next time. And I walked fifteen feet away.

Bingo. The next man talked to her for a minute, his eyes on the ten the whole time. When he walked away, he had the bill in his pocket. Elvia said, "He said to see Orlando Finney."

"I know that much."

"Yeah, well, he says Finney isn't around today."

"I guessed that. I hope you didn't waste ten bucks to find out the only two things I know."

"Why are we looking for him?"

"You ever trade baseball cards in Tocambaro?"

"No."

"When I was a kid, I'd trade for all the Luis Aparicio cards I could get. I traded Mays, Mantle, Banks, Aaron—all of 'em straight up for all the Little Looies I could get my hands on. Other kids thought I was nuts."

"What's that supposed to mean?"

"I'll explain it later. What else did the guy say?"

"He said Finney deals out of a booth at Nate's Delicatessen. You know where that is?"

"Of course."

"He said there's another man in the booth today but he believes the man is working for Finney."

We were at 14th and Morgan. Nate's is on Maxwell. We walked north on Morgan. A black teenager in a long black leather coat and a yellow fedora sidled up to me. He flashed open his coat to show a long gold chain, closed the lapel over it quick. He asked if I wanted to treat my lady and nodded at Elvia. I smiled, said, "Sorry." The kid hurried off.

Elvia said, "Was that hot?"

"No. But he wants you to think that."

"Thanks for the treat."

"Dog's ass PI's are notorious tightwads. I probably should've warned you about that."

Nate's was jammed and noisy. People of all colors, races, and creeds, haggling, arguing and conversing over mugs of Nate's coffee, which is about the best in town. We managed to find a spot at the counter, even though we had to stand. I ordered some of the coffee. Strong black coffee is the perfect partner for amphetamines. Each sip of caffeine gives the speed a little power boost.

I turned and leaned against the counter, surveyed the room. In ninety seconds, I was sure I'd spotted our man. A young Hispanic in the last booth. Wide Indian face, a huge hook nose, thick purplish lips, wearing a Dallas Cowboys baseball cap. He sat by himself. A mug of coffee and a pile of papers was on the table in front of him.

He wasn't alone all the time. His visitors were mostly white men who looked like they were used to giving orders and making money. They would slide into the booth across from him, talk to him for a few seconds, and shove something across the table to him. The kid would shove one of the slips of paper back and the men would leave the booth and Nate's.

I watched the scene play four times, then said, "There's our man," and nodded in his direction.

Nate's was so crowded, it didn't matter if Elvia turned and stared. The kid would never have noticed. She said, "Why are we trying to find Orlando Finney?"

"Business."

"Don't start."

I smiled. So did she. I said, "My plan is still something I'm not sure I wanna do. I'm not sure I can do it, and if I can, I'm not sure it'll work. But if I decide to do it, Finney's whereabouts is like ingredient one."

Elvia made a sour face but didn't push it.

Around noon, the kid started glancing at his watch. His steady stream of customers slacked off. Between 12:30 and 12:45, there were only two. At 1:00, the kid stuffed the remaining papers inside his coat and left the booth, headed for the door.

I motioned to Elvia and we followed. I said, "Keep him out front until I get here with the Skylark."

"How?"

"Tell him you want illegals or you're an illegal who wants to work. Anything."

"What if he ignores me?"

"Say anything that'll keep him here for five minutes. The Skylark's not far."

It took more like ten minutes, but Elvia was a great little liar. The two of them stood out front talking up a storm. I stopped at the light, tapped the horn so she'd know I was there. She glanced my way, gave no sign of recognition. Just like a pro. When the light changed, I squared the block and returned. She was alone.

She ran to the car. Closing the door she said, "He went two blocks south and then went into that alley where the sign says Red Hots."

The alley wasn't big enough for the Skylark so I had to go another block down, make a left.

Onto 18th. It was crowded here, too, and I cursed as I scanned groups of people, fearing I'd lost him. But Elvia said, "There he is." He was half a block ahead of us, striding like an Olympic fast walker.

I stayed four car lengths behind. He walked five blocks. The people and cars thinned and I worried he'd spot us, but he never turned around.

We were in a rundown residential area now. Nineteenth century stone and wood buildings, looking like Medieval hovels. This was one of the many bottom rung neighborhoods that dot the fringes of the Loop. A port of entry for Hispanics just up from Mexico and blacks and whites just up from Mississippi or Appalachia.

Another two blocks and the surroundings got worse. Liquor stores and bars were one to the block here. We got to Canalport and he went right, doubling back. All the way back to Halsted. When we turned onto Halsted, I heard the construction noise up ahead. Jackhammers, heavy truck engines, male voices yelling.

The kid went beyond the construction area where the street was down to one lane. Three doors down from the end of a ditch dug between the street and the sidewalk was a brick drugstore. The kid ducked into a doorway at the side of it.

Next to the drugstore was a pizza parlor with a small lot. I drove into the lot, turned off the ignition. Told Elvia we'd sit tight and wait. But right away the kid scampered back out the door, fear and confusion contorting his face. He didn't even glance around, just took off in a fast trot back the way he came.

All the energy I had, speed created and otherwise, spilled out of me. I felt limp. I muttered, "God*dammit!*"

"What?"

In a tired voice I said, "I'm going up those stairs to make sure, but the odds are that Orlando Finney is dead."

"Jesus."

"I know. I don't think I wanna play this game anymore."

Elvia walked over with me. I didn't bother telling her to go back to the car.

There was one doorway at the top of the stairs. Ancient wood turned gray with chips of white paint speckling it. It was wide open.

We walked into a small kitchen with a high ceiling and appliances circa 1920. Tiny white refrigerator and small stove. White porcelain deep double sink with goose neck faucet. Black and white square tile floor.

We went through that into a sparsely furnished living room and there we found Finney's body. His back was against the front of an orange couch, his head resting on the cushions. He stared at us. There were multiple bullet holes in his chest. Buckets of blood stained the wooden floor beneath him. He'd been alive an hour ago. The blood hadn't started to thicken.

There was nothing to say or do or look for. I said, "Let's go."

I left the front door of the apartment wide open like we'd found it, in case the kid came back with the police. I doubted he would but you never know. When the body was found, my name would come up sooner or later. I didn't want to give anybody an excuse to ask if I'd been here.

We walked slowly back to the Skylark. Elvia said, "Will you please tell me what is going on?"

I put my arm around her shoulder, pulled her close. I said, "I'm not sure. But my plan is shot to hell. Probably a good thing."

"What was it?"

"I was going to turn Finney over to the Kings in exchange for them taking Toreldo out."

"Kill the cop?"

"Yeah. One scumbag for another scumbag. Straight up."

And I was serious about that trade. And being serious gave me a good idea where my head was at. It was not in a good place.

THIRTY–SEVEN

There was nothing to do except drive back to the hotel. I tried to think things out as we went, but my brain had an OUT OF ORDER DUE TO OPERATOR ABUSE sign on it. As usual, the speed ravaged my thought processes, never keen in the best of times. I worked out the Valium bottle from my pants and ate two to buffer the crash.

I wasn't as sure about Finney's murder as I had been about Ford's. There were a bunch of prime suspects for this one. Nicky Toreldo and any one of a hundred ninety-nine Romeo Kings. Finney had been more scared of the Kings when I talked to him the day before; never even mentioned Cantel until after I did. But if he'd known what I knew about Toreldo, I guarantee he'd've changed the billing on that one.

I should've before, but I certainly wasn't running to the law about what I knew now. *Somebody* would warn Toreldo and somebody else would start the coverup. Big city police departments always react to accusations of corruption by circling the wagons. I'd have to go to the Feds to get anything done and they'd take forever. I didn't have forever. Plus, I didn't know how many compadres Toreldo had on the force. Half of Vice could be as crooked as he was for all I knew. I didn't want to get into a position where every time I saw a blue shirt I started freaking out. I was doing enough of that already.

At the hotel, I fed Bugs, then sat on the bed, thinking. Elvia was on the floor, watching the rabbit scamper about. He'd scoot up to her, sniff, hop quickly away. She smiled weakly. I wished I could of. Her eyes on Bugs, she said, "Who killed Finney?"

"Might've been a King. Might've been Toreldo."

She looked at me. Said, "This is like the *rurales* in Mexico. Everybody jokes about how corrupt they are and about their private graveyards. It's because of all the drug money."

"Same with Toreldo. A vice cop his age makes maybe thirty grand a year. He's arresting eighteen-year-old punk kids with almost that much cash in their pockets, gold chains hanging round their necks, tooling around town in Porsches they might of paid cash for. I imagine Toreldo started pondering how unfair that is. When you think about the basic injustice of a situation like that, you start to rationalize. You take a few tiny steps and you get away with it and nobody gets hurt. Then it gets out of hand. Before you know it, you're on the other side. There's just too much money in drugs. Cops're only human."

"He'll get caught."

I shrugged. "Maybe. Someday when it won't help me any. Wearing a badge makes it perfect for him. Dopers won't mess with cops because the consequences are too high, so they'll co-operate. Brother cops cover for you for the most part. The public assumes you're stashing away a little bribe money for those golden years, but they never suspect you've turned into the enemy. He's pretty safe actually."

"Is he going to try and kill us?"

"Me, probably. There's still time for you to vanish. May never knew your name."

I went over and sat next to her. Gave her a hug. The Valiums started to calm me so I ate two more. Elvia put her hand out. I shook out three and neither of us said a word about them making people lazy.

I said, "I'm gonna call Marvin. He goes to the office on Saturday. Maybe somebody called."

Elvia said she was staying with Bugs. I didn't blame her. Nobody wanted to kill Bugs.

Marvin sounded pleasantly detached. Marvin likes a Manhattan or four once in a while, and today was one of those whiles.

I asked if anybody had called.

He said, "Dan, my man, I spent more time at your desk than at my own. I am going to give you a fucking answering machine Monday morning as a gift. You'd think a man who's business keeps him away from his office most of the time would break down and—"

"Marvin, who called?"

"Oh yeah. I wrote 'em down. Hang on." He dropped the receiver. I listened to muffled cursing and then the crackly sound of paper being unfolded, then his voice boomed loud into my ear. "You still with me, Dannyboy?"

He wasn't just detached, he was bombed. He only calls me Dannyboy when he's real messed up because he knows I'm not fond of Dannyboy.

I said, "Still here. Sounds like you need a drink, Marvin."

"Already had a couple." He giggled.

"Really? You sure can hold your liquor. I'd never of guessed."

"Least I ain't a pill popper and a pot smoker on top of being a lush. Dannyboy, I bet you got the insides of a ninety-year-old man. I bet—"

"Marvin, who the fuck called me?"

He laughed some more. "You're such a popular man, Dannyboy. Let's see, there were the two bill collectors. Just jokin'. Luis Santiago called twice. At about nine and again at eleven. And a Nicholas Toreldo."

I said, "Shit."

"Who is this dago?"

"Bad news."

"Mafia type?"

"Worse than a mafia type."

"How can a dago be worse than mafia?"

"Never mind. Orlando Finney didn't call?"

"Just these two."

"What were the messages?"

"Call Santiago. Dan, my man, why you hangin' with all these spic types?" Excessive drink brings out Marvin's true personality. And a primary component of his true personality is a lack of racial tolerance. It's a trait he shares with most of the Northwest Side. He said, "Those gangbanger guys comin' to my office, these guys calling you. And that wetback babe you're with all the time. You into that yet?"

"Marvin, nip it. How about Toreldo?"

"Yeah, a damn dago gangster. See what I'm talking about?"

"I mean did he leave a message?"

"Just that he called and he'd be getting in touch."

My stomach went cold as a freezer, but at least I knew for sure May had spilled her guts before she died. I said, "Okay, thanks. Have a Manhattan on me."

"Splendid idea, Dannyboy." Marvin was laughing like hell. Such a good, safe, jolly business, the insurance business.

THIRTY–EIGHT

My address book is ripped pieces of paper and matchbook covers with phone numbers scribbled on them stuffed in my wallet and pockets. Eventually, I found two numbers for Santiago. No answer at the first. A woman, speaking Spanish, answered the second. Switching immediately to English, she said it was one of the community groups Santiago directed. He wasn't there either, but I laid on the charm and she gave me his home number.

I asked what was up.

He said, "I'm just curious about how you're doing on the Reyes murder."

"I wish I never laid eyes on Elvia Reyes."

"She that bad?"

"Personally I like her fine, but if I'd never seen her, I wouldn't be involved with so many dead bodies."

"How many dead bodies besides Ricardo we talking about?"

I silently totaled stiffs, then wondered what I should tell Santiago. I didn't trust anybody for shit anymore. I was as paranoid as Richard Nixon. The speed crash exacerbated it. I decided some of the story I could safely relate, some I'd play dumb about. I said, "Counting Ricardo, eight. I think."

Santiago whistled. "Eight? Sweet Jesus, who's killing these people?"

"I don't know."

"You got suspicions?"

I thought, yeah, a boatload, but I said, "No."

"You must have *some* idea."

"None, Luis. All I know is it's drug related and you know as well as I that nowadays druggies blast away soon as they suspect something's fishy."

"I thought Finney was dealing illegals, not drugs."

"Somewhere along the line he crossed over."

"You mentioned Joseph Cantel to me the other day. I asked around about him. He's involved in this?"

"He's hiding out so I guess so. What'd you learn?"

"Only that he deals heavy drugs like heroin and cocaine."

"I already knew that."

"I know. Who are the other dead people?"

I hesitated, figured what the hell. It'd all been in the papers. Or would be. I said, "Stacey Ford and his girlfriend. You know Ford?"

"No."

"He was an Okie who thought he was Lex Luthor. He started pitting lowlifes against each other. It didn't work, he only lasted a week."

"Who else?"

"Orlando Finney."

"You serious?"

"As a heart attack. Happened this morning. I don't think the police know it yet."

"Daniel, you must have some idea what's going on."

"I don't, but if I did, what do you care?"

"This kind of thing affects the Hispanic community. Drugs and gangs are major problems down here. You know that."

I said, "Speaking of that, I talked to Ricky Medina yesterday. The Kings are looking to be *the* major cocaine boys in town."

"He told you that?"

"Uh huh. He wanted me to finger Finney for him so they could uphold Romeo King honor. I refused, but somebody found him. Might've been them."

Santiago said, "That's interesting because another reason I wanted to talk to you was to tell you what I heard this morning. Two Kings were murdered last night on 18th and Carpenter. Everybody assumed it was a drive-by, but today I heard stories that it was the Kings themselves who took these two out."

"Kings killing Kings?"

"Bizarre, right? Then I remembered how you thought a King had found that money in Ricardo's room."

"I'm not sure I believe that anymore."

"Did you tell your theory about it to them?"

"To Medina and his scarfaced shadow, yeah."

"See what I'm getting at? If you told them that enough times and seemed pretty sure you believed it, they might've started to wonder."

"It's possible. Know the names of these two?"

"The *Trib's* got two paragraphs on it. You ever notice how with murders Latinos get two paragraphs, Uptown whites and blacks get three, and yuppies get half a page with photos?"

"Yuppies are the only ones who read these papers. Got to check the stock market. Probably just the opposite in *La Raza.*"

He chuckled. Said, "It says here Francisco Delgado, 18, of blah blah blah, and Miguel Gonzalez, 22. Let's see, found about ten o'clock on the northwest corner of 18th and Carpenter. Neighbors said they heard a volley of shots shortly before. But in that neighborhood, who pays attention to gunfire? Last sentence says police suspect the murders are gang related."

"There's some astute detective work. Teenage Hispanics gunned down on a street corner in Pilsen. How *did* they figure it was gang related? Who told you it was Kings?"

"People in the know."

"Any chance you could find out if one of these two was the King who ran up the stairs at the Elizabeth Hotel and found Ricardo Reyes' dead?"

"Only if I got very lucky. Neither you or I would get an answer to a question like that from anybody who really knows. I only thought this would be something you'd like to know and I wanted to see how you were doing on the Reyes thing. It sounds like not good."

"Not good sums it up real well. And thanks."

"Sure thing, amigo."

I right away called Medina's number. Not there. The man who answered said he'd be back "soon." I said I'd call until he showed.

I sat at the counter and sipped more black coffee. The caffeine mixed with the Valium and they made a passable up-down shock absorber.

I wondered if Santiago was right. Maybe I *was* responsible for the two Kings getting hit. It didn't bother me, but it did make me curious. And puzzled. About a lot of things. But when your brain habitually cruises with the energy of a turtle on quaaludes, a state of puzzlement is more or less the status quo.

It was over an hour—eight smoked-down-to-the-brown Kools, four cups of coffee and sugar, and four phone calls—before Medina answered the phone.

I asked, "The Finney deal still open?"

"It is."

"What am I getting out of it?"

"The unending friendship of the Romeo Kings."

"Could you make that undying?"

"If you'd like."

"I thought when you said worth my while we were talking cash."

He was quiet for a bit. Then he said, "You know where he is or not?"

I said, "You don't seem near as agitated about it as you did yesterday."

"I got other things on my mind now."

"So I hear. Plus maybe you don't need the information anymore."

No answer.

"Level, Enrique. He's dead. How'd you guys find him?"

"Who says we did?"

"You had the biggest reason for wanting him dead."

"Doesn't mean we did it. The man had mucho enemies."

"I know that," I said. "What's the other problem you got now?"

"It's personal."

I was still looking to deal, so I said, "Maybe I can help."

He thought about it. "Maybe."

"I charge a fee you know."

He said, "You got a pencil? Write down this address." He read a Little Village number. Said, "It's not in Pilsen, which means it's out of King territory so it's not like you'll have to worry for your safety. Meet me there at four o'clock."

"Just you, Enrique. If I get the creeps when I see the place, I'm gone. I won't even stop the car."

"Quit worryin'. If I wanted to take you out, you'd of been dead meat long time ago. We've had plenty of chances."

THIRTY–NINE

I called Stefan Constantine from the coffee shop next to the hotel. Stefan is a Greek-American cop I've kept in touch with since academy days. Not being much brighter than me, it'd taken him fifteen years to make plainclothes. Then a year ago, he'd gone over his superiors' heads on a double homicide and now he pushed paper into file cabinets all day at the Englewood station. Got assigned to thirty-year-old murders to see if he could shake some clues loose. To cops, that kind of job is hilarious unless it's you doing it.

We talked baseball for a minute, then I said, "I'm calling about a narcotics cop on the take."

His voice was cold and impersonal when he answered. "Yeah? You mean we got cops on the take in Chicago?"

"Shocking, I know. It's important."

"You want the Office of Professional Standards."

"I'm not interested in pitching a bitch. Just need some information. If you've got it."

"Listen, Dan, I don't conduct conversations like this on the phone. Where you at?"

I told him the address. Said, "I'll be here at least an hour."

He said he was on his way.

He walked through the door forty minutes later. He looked the same as he did twenty years ago when we were both young and brainless. The face was a little more saggy and a lot more worn, but he was still skinnier than me, still wore his hair in a 50's style butch cut, still had the perpetual five o'clock shadow, and his eyes still zipped every which way constantly, like a fly caught between window panes. He never could dress worth a damn. His trenchcoat made Columbo's look like a brand new Burberry and his tie was as wide as a towel. A cigar hung from his mouth. It would never be lit.

Constantine made me slide from the booth so he could pat me down.

I said, "I'm not wired."

"Sorry, but I read the papers and see the State's Attorney making noises about police corruption and then you just happen to call me and start asking about narcs on the take. I realize we go back to the Stone Age days, but I know how that asshole works. I ain't testifyin' in court in no cop show scandal, pointing my finger at some poor schmuck who takes a twenty now and then just so that asshole can get reelected. I got enough problems."

"It's cool."

When we were back in the booth, he said, "Who's the slimeball?"

"Nicholas Toreldo."

"God."

"Know him?"

"Heard of him."

I had to proceed cautiously here. Constantine might pretend to be scared to death of the State's Attorney, but he might also be stuffing crooked money into his bank account faster than Toreldo, so I didn't want to detail my troubles. I said, "He seems a bit more bent than the average vice cop supplementing his paycheck."

"That's possible."

I said, "Come on, Stefan, open up. This is important to me. You know this conversation is not taking place."

He chuckled low in his throat. Shifted the cigar from one side of his mouth to the other. His eyes surveyed the ceiling. He said, "Okay, Daniel, for old times sake and seeing as you swear you ain't looking to mix me up in no scandal, I'll confirm for you." He took the cigar from his mouth and looked at it for a long second, then looked at me. Said, "Toreldo is the worst piece of garbage to flash a badge I've heard of in seventeen years on the job. He doesn't even hide it much. Brags about it. He expects his compadres will always cover for him. They have so far, but if you keep pushing—. And he's vicious, Daniel. Like a human pit bull. Sadistic, actually. That helps because it makes the younger officers afraid of him." He put the cigar back in his mouth and resumed casing the ceiling.

We were silent for a few seconds. I reflected again on how easy it is for a cop to go off the straight. For various reasons, nobody wants to jerk your chain. If you can cop to the disgrace in your head you got it made.

Constantine smiled. Said, "Hey, Daniel, remember when we started. That was what? Sixteen, seventeen years ago?"

"About."

"Hell, we palmed a sawbuck here and there, right?"

"Sure, everybody did."

"Of course. The cops, the lawyers, the inspectors. Back then it was part of the job. The old boys showed us rookies how to do it right the first week on the street. It was no big deal."

"Toreldo goes way beyond taking a twenty to ignore a bag of pot in the glove compartment or fifty to let a saloon keep a chippie in the back room."

"I know, Daniel." Constantine was genuinely embarrassed. I couldn't tell if from being on the same police force as a pig like Toreldo or because I called him for rationalizing for the guy.

I said, "I'm hearing that not only does he take, he uses and deals. Coke for sure, maybe harder than that. And obviously he don't have to worry about finding a connection."

"I've heard that."

"Heroin?"

"Anything's possible."

I said, "I hear he keeps his supply ample shaking dealers down and raiding the evidence room."

Looking over my shoulder he said, "I'm aware how he does it."

"So why isn't he discreet about it?"

"He probably was at first. But as time went by maybe he got to feeling like King Kong. Who's going to turn him in? Not the dealers. 'Hey, I want to report this asshole, he's stealing my cocaine.'"

"What about you?"

"*I* don't need the aggravation. Like I said, I got my own troubles."

"Know anything about him personally?"

"We don't work together. Thank God."

"Anybody else in vice like him."

"I suppose." The eyes clouded over. He said, "You really sound like you're working for the fuckin' state, Daniel. You better not involve me in any bullshit."

"I'm asking only because Toreldo is gunning for me."

"Honest?"

"Honest."

"Jeezus. All I know is what you obviously know."

"He got a family?"

"This is what I hear, okay? I don't know him personally, but people I know do. His wife left him after he beat the tar out of her once too often. Three years ago about. Since then is when he really tossed it in. Stopped giving a shit. He's got a son about eight. Sees him on weekends. Man loves the kid. Hard to figure, I know. I mean he's one of those fathers brags the kid up constantly, dragging out the photos of the little bastard and all that. And supposedly he's a totally different man around the kid. Takes him fishing, to the ballgame, they go to Lincoln Park Zoo. He's like Ward Cleaver or something. I was told he says he'll kill anybody who even looks cross-eyed at the kid. And the boy worships Toreldo. Thinks his old man is like J. Edgar Hoover and Steve Garvey rolled into one. Of course, the clincher is that old

Nicholas will get his ass nailed one of these days and he'll end up hurting the kid ten times worse than anybody else ever could. Toreldo is too fucking stupid to figure that out."

We sipped coffee. I lit another Kool, blew out a nervous lungful of smoke. I said, "Toreldo might be dead soon."

Constantine's eyes stopped swerving and stuck on mine for a second, then dropped down. He didn't say anything for a bit. Then he whispered, "Not you, Daniel. Don't tell me that."

"Not me, Stefan. He's got some cocaine gangs pissed at him." Close enough to the truth.

"You know these gangs?"

"Kind of. Suppose they ask, what can I tell 'em?"

"Tell 'em killing a cop is killing a cop, even a sleazeball cop. I'll admit Homicide wouldn't break down doors to solve Nicholas Toreldo's murder, but he's still a cop. They wouldn't blow it off, that's for sure."

"I'm not saying it'll happen. Just that there's a point where even a badge can't—" I trailed off, feeling embarrassed.

Constantine suddenly slid from the booth, shaking his head. He tossed a crumpled fin on the table. Said, "This conversation depresses me, Daniel. I don't wanna hear no more." He walked out of the coffee shop still shaking his head.

I sat there, staring into my cup of coffee, remembering the look on Constantine's face when it dawned on him what I was saying. Suddenly I knew I couldn't do the trade. Even if it was my only way out. It upsets me that I even thought I could.

FORTY

I walked back to the hotel. Elvia was gone. There was a note on her bed. It took me a minute to decipher she was taking a walk and would be back soon. At the bottom of her note, I wrote that I was going for a drive and I'd be back soon, too.

I drove to the Little Village section on the West Side. Down

Kedzie after Cermak, I turned right on 24th. Rows of brick three-stories and tarpaper shingle houses; gang logos spray painted on everything. Little Village ran Pilsen a close second in gangbangers. Soon the brick and tarpaper stopped and the houses got smaller and drabber. More vacant lots. Medina's address was a stone garage so old it had probably once been a horse stable. I stopped and surveyed the area. Across the street was an abandoned two-story brick factory building. Smallish, it had been one of those light industry type of places that kept the local housewives and high-schoolers employed. Fifty yards beyond the factory was a Ma and Pa grocery store with a plywood front window that had prices written on it in magic marker. The rest of the block on both sides was vacant lots full of garbage. Not just refuse but thrown away mattresses and appliances and furniture. It looked like a city dump.

In front of the factory building, six Hispanic men were sitting in and on a Pontiac Bonneville. They were unshaven and all wore baseball caps and denim jackets over black T-shirts. Each one had a cigarette sticking out of his mouth and held a brown bag with bottle mouth protruding out the top. One stood while I looked them over and started swaying to the beat of Salsa music that boomed from a beat box perched on the roof of the car. They didn't wear King colors, but there had to be a connection. I doubted they'd consider it necessary to show a great deal of courtesy to a strange gringo so I didn't bother to ask any questions. I decided to drive around the block until Medina showed up. The scenery was too enticing to pass up. Twelve hostile eyes watched me drive off.

My sixth trip around, at five after four, Medina was standing alone in front of the double doors of the garage. He didn't look like anything close to a big time coke man. He wore a baggy green T-shirt that rode up over his belly, baggy blue jeans and gray hightops with lime green laces. These guys should've consulted a fashion designer before they chose their colors. Then again, with so many gangs in town, these might've been the only colors left.

When I pulled to the curb, Medina waddled to the car and bent to talk into the passenger window, resting his blubbery arms on the sill. I said, "I ain't likin' the six muchachos over there. They make me nervous."

"Don't worry about those guys. I snap my fingers and they are—" He leaned back and slapped his palms together, shooting his right hand out like a jet taking off.

"So snap."

"They don't do nothing unless they hear the order from me. In me you have the perfect bodyguard."

"Where's their green and gray?"

He fingered the tiny tuft of hair below his lip. "This ain't a King area. I told you that. Remember what I said about the gangs that are eager to join up with us?" He nodded across the street. That's one of 'em."

"Rand McNally's not inside?"

Enrique made a noise like he was getting irritated. "There will be me and you and two teenage girls inside. I think maybe you and me could take care of the girls should they decide to get tough. Are you fucking coming in with me so we can talk or not? I told you on the phone you'd be a dead man ten times over if I wanted you out of the way. But I don't. I'm a businessman and we can do business."

I got out of the car and did my best Bogart walk across the sidewalk that was precious little concrete and a lot dirt to the double doors. Medina unlocked four locks with four different keys and pushed the door open with his shoulder.

He didn't tell me the teenage girls would be naked. And sackin'. The girls stood under two fluorescent lights to the left of the doors in front of a long table piled high with packages wrapped in butcher paper and filament tape. They looked at me looking at them and there was no change of expression on their faces. We watched them work. They'd open one of the packages, stick a tiny plastic Baskin-Robbins spoon inside it, then pour the brown powder the spoon brought out into a red or blue balloon. They folded the balloon over and under and tied it shut. They dropped the folded balloon, now the size of a bullet, onto a card table behind them.

Medina said, "A benefit, man. Girls just up from Mexico. Don't know a word of English. It's got to be bare assed or they'd walk off with so much dope there'd be nothing left to sell. And they don't mind because it pays good. I got a older sister who thinks she's above all this. She sticks Clorox and bologna into sacks at a Eagle store in Pilsen. Makes six fucking bucks an hour, looks down on the rest of the family 'cause she's 'honest' and we're criminals." He paused, shook his head in wonder. "Dumb, eh?"

After a minute, I looked around the rest of the garage. Four white windowless vans were jammed side by side in the area between where the girls worked and the other wall. They had Texas plates and stickers. There was an overwhelming gasoline smell and something else. A bitter, acrid smell, like the sourest sweat.

Medina nudged me. Said, "See the balloons. I used to sell those. Took care of my people. Now *I* distribute."

I said, "This is heroin, Enrique. I thought you said free base cocaine is the wave of the future, this stuff is passé."

Medina shrugged, smiled wide as Vanna White. "When a money-making opportunity drops in your lap, what do you say? Sorry, no, I prefer cocaine? No way. You take it and add it to what you already got. I realize heroin doesn't provide access to the beautiful people and the giant money, but it's got that loyal clientele."

He led me toward the girls. He said something in Spanish and they stepped away from the table. They both leaned against the stone wall, kept their eyes on the oily cement floor.

Medina picked up one of the larger, paper-wrapped packages. A shaky 'C' was written on the side of it with black magic marker. He said, "This is the poor quality stuff. The C means it's not very pure." He tossed it down, picked up two more packets, one in each hand. One had a 'B' on it, the other an 'A'. "Better and best," he said, smiling, holding one up, then the other. "Like buying a stove at Sears, dig? Our budget model, our better model, our best model. Some junkies can afford better Henry than others, some got a bigger Jones." He set the packets down, put a finger up like he was scolding me. "But not top of the line." He went to the end of the table. A white foam cooler sat there. He opened it and took out a lumpy, softball sized paper wrapped packet. A 'P' was scrawled on it. "P stands for pure, man," he said.

He laid it on the table in front of me, slit the tape with a pen knife the girls had been using, and peeled the paper away. He motioned me to look at it. The dope was black and looked like tar on a driveway before it's flattened and hardens. I whistled as Medina beamed. I didn't know how much heroin was in the package, but an ounce of industrial strength heroin fetches a minimum of five grand on the street. In hard times, right after a major bust, twice that probably wouldn't be enough.

I said, "I could make me a bundle from CrimeStoppers, calling in this address."

Medina kept smiling. I didn't blame him. If just a small portion of the money from the drugs in this garage ended up in his wallet, he had plenty to smile about. He said, "You'd never do that. I know you too well now, Dan. You live and let live. That's your philosophy and that's a good philosophy to have."

I nodded. "I don't blame any man for tryin' to get over however he can. But I'm very confused about why you're showing me all this."

The smile vanished, Medina's face got serious. "I was impressed by how fast you found Orlando Finney."

"Wasn't as fast as you."

"Perhaps that was another one of those opportunities that got dropped in my lap. But you did it on smarts or ability or whatever it is you street cops got."

"Guile, Enrique, born of desperation."

"Well, you got some kind of knack. You know the streets, you know the procedures. I got another job I need done and I wanted to prove to you first that I wasn't blowing smoke the other day in the restaurant. The Romeo Kings are going to be big. Bigger than anybody now or before. And I am the leader of the Romeo Kings. I'm gonna have so much money and power I'm gonna be like Al Capone in this town."

"Learn from the past, Medina, pay your taxes."

"I'm serious."

"No doubt. A man's got to dream big."

He waved his hand. "This is no dream. It will happen. Being the leader of the Kings, I'd be in a position to see that some of that money rolls your way. You know Chicago like very few people. You can go anywhere. You work fast. Hook up with us."

"And do what? Deal bags of smack?"

"You'll never have to touch the dope. You tough?"

"Not very."

"Good. I know lots of tough guys who got brains like a jackass. I need a man who can operate. You know where DuPrey is?"

DuPrey is a blue collar town fifty miles from Chicago. A dying blue collar town. Lots of unemployment, lots of crime, lots of bars and flop hotels.

I said, "I've been there, but I try not to stay long."

"Follow me." He spoke Spanish to the girls. As we walked away they went back to the table.

He led me to the back of the garage, unlocked and pushed through a wooden door. Before I followed Medina, I took one last look at the girls. I said, "The job wouldn't be supervising the girls would it? I'll take it if it is."

Medina said, "I know you would but what would I do?"

Behind the door was a small office as messy and cluttered as the vacant lots up and down the block. Taking up most of the room was an ancient executive type desk. The top of it was so chipped and pitted it would've been impossible to write a legible sentence on a piece of paper laying on it. The desk's right front leg was gone, replaced with a Sears catalog, so the desk sloped slightly toward the door. Behind the desk was a huge tilt and swivel chair older than me and dirtier than the garage floor. A black vinyl-bottomed lounge chair sat between the desk and the right wall. The vinyl was all sliced up and urethane foam was crawling out and over the seat. Behind the desk hung old posters advertising Spanish dances. A shelf ran around the room at chest level with trophies standing here and there. Above the shelf the walls were painted sea green, vertical wood paneling ran from shelf to floor.

Medina sat behind the desk, said, "Sit in the black chair, Dan." like he was offering me a throne. When I sat down, he said "I asked about DuPrey because I want to hire you to go there."

"You'd *have* to pay me to go there."

"I want you to bring somebody back for me."

"This somebody want to come back?"

"He most certainly does not."

"Get him yourself."

"Can't do it, Dan. Let me set the scene for you. DuPrey is twenty percent Mex and they got plenty of gangs. The man I need is hiding with a gang that is affiliated with an enemy of ours. We'd never get near him."

"Send someone he doesn't know."

"That's what I'm trying to do."

"I mean a King or a friend of the Kings."

"He was a King. He knows us, he knows our friends."

"Send one of those guys across the street."

He held up his index and second finger. "One, those boys across the street are eager and they're mean, but they are dumber than livestock and they don't know DuPrey from Milwaukee. Two, I know you do good work. As long as you don't get too fucked up."

I said, "You know where he is?"

"The very house. But we got no allies out there. Not yet anyway. None of us would get close to the house. If we did, he'd never come out. If we wait around for him, they'd bring the DuPrey cops down on us or jump us themselves. He'd never suspect a gringo."

"How'd you learn the address?"

"Don't worry about that."

"I need to know details like that before I take a job."

"Trust me on this. Its legit. I wouldn't even make the offer unless I was positive he was there."

"This the kid who popped the two Kings?"

"Might be."

"He a King?"

"Was."

"How will I know him? I might bring back the wrong guy."

"I've got photos. You'll have the address. It shouldn't be too hard. You're a detective, you know how to do these things. Actually, I don't care how you do it, just so you bring him back."

"I won't kill him."

"I know. I don't want you to. And it pays well, Dan. I can offer top dollar now."

I was shaking my head as he spoke the last bit. Said, "If I do it, I don't want money."

He looked at me, sorely puzzled. Money figured into every equation of his life. He'd probably never heard the words 'I don't want money' before.

I said, "You appear to be The Boy in this place now."

Medina didn't want to grin, but he was so pleased with himself he did anyway. "That could be," he said.

"Then what I want for my fee is for you to call a vice cop named Toreldo. The man's looking to kill me."

"I won't kill a cop if that's what your fee is."

"That's not it. Yesterday I thought about it, but I just can't put a contract out on somebody. Not even this piece of slime. This Toreldo is a druggie and so crooked he makes a boomerang look straight. Tell him what you told me. The new connection, how big you're gonna get. Tell him you'll deal with him if he'll provide some legal muscle. People who hook up with him tend to not get busted. He can tell you lots of inside stuff and help out with the rough stuff."

"So what's in that for you?"

"Then you tell him he's part of the operation and *I'm* part of the operation. And then I want to talk to him with you present. I talk to him alone, I'm a dead man before I open my mouth to pitch my plea."

"I'm awful distrustful of cops, even if they are crooked."

"Toreldo has a badge, but he's no cop. He's vicious as hell. He uses drugs, sells 'em, protects dealers he likes and shakes down the ones he don't. He's been working with a heroin dealer downtown. I don't think it's anything like what you're setting up. He'll probably jump at the chance to be part of a bigger operation."

Medina pulled on his lower lip. Said, "I dunno, a cop."

"It's my only chance, Enrique. I've got to talk to him and I got to have a mediator. Imply to him that I'm one of the good guys and you wouldn't want to see anything bad happen to me. Like my death. Lean on him for me. Then let me have my say. That's the fee.

"You'll bring back my man if I say yes?"

"Of course."

"Wait outside. Let me make a call."

I went into the garage, lit a cigarette, watched the slim fawn-colored girls shift heroin from packet to balloon. They both looked over, saw I was staring, didn't give a shit. It all paid the same. You came to work, took your clothes off, poured dope into color coded balloons and sometimes a skinny gringo checked your boobs and ass out.

I pondered what I was doing. Asked myself where in hell did I go wrong in life. Dragging a gangbanger back to most likely get snuffed, begging a favor from a heroin dealer, and arranging it all in a stinking garage in a neighborhood that belonged in Guatemala. A homeless wino sleeping one off on Lower Wacker probably had higher self-esteem than I did at the moment.

I walked to one of the vans, opened the back door. The nauseating smell that drifted faintly through the garage rushed at me like a boxer's punch. I gagged and slammed the door shut. One of the girls giggled. I walked quickly away from the vans to the other side of the garage and leaned against a table adjacent to the girl's table. My table was full of blackened mechanics tools and twisted metal parts covered with sludgy grease.

Two minutes later, Enrique emerged from the office. "You got a deal," he said quietly. He handed me a legal size envelope. Said, "There are five photos of Cesar Lopez in here and the address he is at. I'll be waiting for your call."

He went back into the office.

FORTY–ONE

On the way back to the hotel, I chainsmoked Kools and thought as hard as my chemical-addled brain can think. I figured out two things. At least I hoped I figured out two things, but I couldn't see it any other way.

The vans in the garage were *las trocas*, the illegal's taxi service Elvia had told me about. The smell that filled the vans so completely that it wafted out and overpowered the gasoline saturated air of a decades old garage was the smell of dirt poor people who were scared, completely powerless, and facing a future in a new world that they knew didn't want any part of them.

When I thought of illegal aliens these days, I immediately thought of Orlando Finney. I'd bet big bucks if I had any that Finney had been in that garage on many occasions—daily, perhaps.

Also in that garage was the heroin. And because of what I'd learned the last week that made me think of Joseph Cantel.

Illegal aliens and heroin both come from Mexico. I thought how convenient and economical it would be to ship them together.

So I pieced it together, slowly, concentrating on every little thing I knew so far. Finney had been operating the wetback taxicabs for years, on top of being a well-known small-timer. It would be solid business for him to be approached by either Cantel or someone on behalf of Cantel and asked to move heroin to Chicago in the vans with the illegals. Let an illegal smuggle the dope across the Grande, put the illegal and the dope in a taxicab van, drive both to Chicago. Give a little—or a lot— of money to Finney for the use of the hall. And the best thing about the scheme was that nobody had to worry about a bust from the time the dope left Mexico until it hit the garage on 24th except the poor "donkey" who was holding. And for a free ride in a taxi that was costing everybody else in it a ton of pesos, that "donkey" would take the risk with his mouth shut tight.

I hit my cigarette hand on the steering wheel. Damn, I am smart sometimes. I smell a little fear-sweat, see some heroin, next thing you know I got a case solved. I deduce that Finney and Cantel were actually partners after hours of wondering what the connection was. I smiled, laughed out loud. I was as impressed as hell with myself for ten minutes.

But the smile faded when I started to wonder why such a perfect partnership bottomed out so quickly. Finney was dead; his junior partner, Ford, was dead; Cantel was hiding out after killing four of *his* junior partners—the ones Ford had turned him on to; and now Cantel's cop was blowing away anybody who knew anything. Anything at all. And God help me, I knew more than anybody.

And there was another puzzle. Enrique Medina was all of a sudden The Man in the garage on 24th. That intrigued me most of all. Who was behind him? Who was putting all this in motion and deciding Medina was big-time material? Medina had tons of ambition and decent enough smarts for a gangbanger but he was no Al Capone by a mile. Just how did a street punk progress from pushing balloons of cheap Henry to derelict junkies in Pilsen one month to Hot Shot at a major Midwest heroin distribution center the next? With plans to add cocaine to the enterprise. Who was making this illogical event happen?

As I twirled that around in my head, my genius deserted me, so I let the thoughts go. One shouldn't expect caviar from a carp.

Elvia was in the room, on hands and knees on the floor, playing with Bugs. She asked where I'd been.

I said, "When you came up from Mexico in the van—"

"I came up from San Antonio in the van. I walked from Mexico to Pearsall. Got a ride from Pearsall to San Antonio."

"Right, the hired killer guy. Where'd you end up?"

She frowned, looked confused. "Chicago."

"Where in Chicago?"

"A garage."

"In Little Village? Twenty-fourth street?"

"Yep."

I smiled.

"Why? What difference does it make?"

"Means this PI can still put two and two together occasionally. Orlando Finney meet you there?"

"No." She stared at me, still wondering what I was getting at. "Some other man."

"Who?"

"I don't know. It was a long time ago. I never saw him again."

"When did you first meet Finney?"

"I don't know."

"Right away?"

"No, but I don't remember when it was."

I sat on the bed, watched Bugs a minute. Said, "I've got a job out of town."

"Where?"

"DuPrey. I'm bringing somebody back for Enrique Medina. I'll go out tomorrow morning."

"Will it take long?"

"I hope not, but it might."

"I'm going too."

I shook my head. "I don't think so. This might take a long time and it might be dangerous. I wouldn't of hired on, but I can't pass up the fee."

She stood, fast and graceful, slinked close and draped her arms around my neck. She kissed me long and soft, gently tapping her hips into mine. After the kiss, she whispered, her lips on mine, "Remember who your partner is?"

"I remember."

"Then I should go."

"Bugs is my partner too, but he's not going."

She put her mouth by my ear, whispered, "Never tell him, but Bugs isn't the bravest or smartest rabbit in the world."

"The job's got nothing to do with your money."

She giggled. Softly bit my neck. "That's okay. You might need a translator if you're going to DuPrey."

She nibbled my neck some more and I shivered and laughed. I said, "I hadn't thought of that. Guess you'll have to go."

We spent the evening exploring each other. Later, in the night—2:00 A.M., when I always jerk awake like a zombie—I sat with my back against the headboard. I turned the lamp on low, studied the photos Medina had given me of Cesar Lopez.

There were two snapshots taken at a party or family get together. He had a happy, festive look on his face. He sat on a sofa with two other men whose faces were blacked out with magic marker. In one, he stared face on into the camera, in the other, he was looking at something to his right. Head-on, profile. Just like a wanted poster.

There were two photos taken outdoors. Lopez wore a blue suit in one, jeans and a black windbreaker over a white knit shirt in the other. He didn't look like a King or any kind of gangbanger. He was dark, had thin lips that struggled to conceal protruding front teeth and he sported a wispy mustache-in-training. His hair was wavy black cut short and combed straight back. It shined brilliantly in the outdoor photos like he had saturated it with lard.

I looked at the indoor profile photo again. It was my favorite because it showed why I couldn't miss getting the right guy. He had a purplish birthmark low on his left check, roughly the size of a quarter. I'd been worrying I'd bring the wrong man back to Medina. That would've been embarrassing considering he had such a high regard for my abilities.

Elvia struggled awake, asked me what was going on. I showed her the photos, said, "Know this guy?"

She took one of the indoor snaps, put it close to her face and leaned over me because the light was on my side of the bed we were sharing. She said, "No. Why are you awake?"

I twisted the lamp knob up higher, gave her the other three photos. "Look at all of them. You sure you don't know him?"

"I'm sure. Is this who we bring back tomorrow?"

"Yes."

"But why are you awake?"

I said, "It's 2:00 A.M. I get a nightly wake up call at 2:00 A.M.. I think it's from the part of my brain that demands to know why I'm such a fuck up. It wants me to ponder the errors of my life and feel depressed about it. Maybe it thinks it can scare me into getting my act together making me worry about such things at 2:00 A.M. Nobody likes the big question at 2:00 A.M."

"You're not so bad. I've met lots worse men."

"Considering the men you know, that's not such a compliment."

"What's that supposed to mean?"

"Never mind. Go back to sleep."

She did, almost immediately, making raspy little snores.

I slipped out of our bed and lay down on the other one. I pulled Bug's cage up from the floor between the beds and set it next to me. Bugs shifted and blinked a lot, then he went back to sleep too. There was still a lot of brandy left from the night before. I lit a Kool and started to sip from the bottle. I twisted the lamp off and lay in the darkness, drinking and smoking. I started reviewing everything that had happened since the moment Elvia had entered my office. I worked my way forward, hour by hour.

I was uneasy about something. It wasn't Toreldo, it was something else. Something *connected*, something in the back of my mind. Something I already *knew*. I stayed with it.

At 4:00 A.M. I fingered it. Immediately rejected it. Didn't like it, didn't want to believe it. Then I replayed everything using this new angle and it all made perfect sense. I knew I was right, but, boy, did I not like it.

At least now I'd sleep.

FORTY–TWO

The next morning, the sky was low and gray and it was so cold I wore two t-shirts under my jacket. At 6:30, Elvia and I sat hunched and shivering in the front seat of the Skylark, waiting for it to warm up. We wrapped hands around giant styrofoam cups of black coffee. The bitter coffee smell filled the car.

As we sat there, Elvia said, "You know, on television I see private detectives wearing suits and ties and they got their hair cut nice. You look like a street person half the time. You'd probably make more money if you dressed better, cleaned up a bit."

I glanced at myself in the rearview mirror. It *was* gruesome I had to admit. But I was still half asleep and a little hungover, so I mumbled, "For Chrissakes, Elvia, TV actors make more in a week than I make in a year. Chill out about that shit."

I had to believe Toreldo wasn't watching the office twenty-four hours a day, especially not at 7:00 A.M. on Sunday. I drove past it three times, going two blocks on either side to flush him out if he was there. I parked in the lot, walked briskly through the sharp air, slipped inside.

From the bottom drawer of my file cabinet, I removed a small black can of mace, the two pair of handcuffs I own, and my baton, left over from my brief law enforcement career. It's a foot-long stick of hard wood with a braided leather loop running through and hanging down from a hole bored into the handle grooves. I never used it as a cop and only one time as a PI. I hardly ever carry it, but not owning a gun means I need some kind of defense weapon on occasion.

Back in the Skylark, I washed down three whites. I asked Elvia if she ever ate speed.

"Sometimes."

"Want some? Might be a long day."

"No. It makes my hair itch and I always throw up. I'll take one of the other ones though. That stuff makes me nervous." She pointed at the stick, the cuffs, and the can on the seat between us.

I shook one out for her. Said, "You know, I plan to quit doing all this shit one of these days. The stuff keeps getting cheaper. In the old days they had pharmaceutical speeds, you had the great cruises and no crash. You came off it like a mother laying a baby in a crib. This garbage is like Dick Butkus running wild in an opponent's backfield. But I'm going to quit."

"If you don't, you'll die."

"That's what I hear."

"Why'd you change beds last night?"

"It bother you?"

"I'm not upset, just curious."

"I had to think."

"You can't think next to me?"

"Next to you I think the wrong kind of thoughts."

"You were thinking about all this stuff that's happened?"

"Yes."

"You have the answers."

"I think so."

"What are they?"

"I'm not a hundred percent sure so I'll wait to talk about it. If I'm right it's too depressing to talk about anyway."

"You won't say *any*thing?"

"Well, one thing. Remember last night I said this job had nothing to do with your money?"

She nodded.

"Maybe I was wrong. I don't think this Cesar Lopez is the man who shot the two Kings. I don't know if Cesar Lopez is even Cesar Lopez. I do think he's the man who sliced up your brother and took the bag of money."

Elvia turned on the seat, facing me. I glanced over. Her eyes were narrow, intense. She said, "Tell me more."

"No."

"Will we get the money back then?"

"I doubt it. The job is to take the man back to Medina. First reasonable chance that presents itself, that's what I do. Unless he has the money on him, which I doubt, we don't get it. I sure as hell am not storming the house he's hiding in."

I could feel Elvia girding for battle. She said, "But if he's got the money hidden in there—"

"It stays there."

"Why do you believe this?"

"I remembered something and because when I sort out what's happened, it's the only way it makes sense."

"You can't tell me?"

"Later."

We left the city, got on the interstate. Because it was Sunday morning, traffic was light and an hour later we entered DuPrey.

It was worse than I remembered. Look up Rust Belt in the dictionary and odds are there's a picture of DuPrey. Just inside the limits was a huge heavy-industry complex that ran for a block. Rusted chains were wrapped around the employees gate and three cold smokestacks eyed the sky.

Past that was a welfare class neighborhood. Blocks of grungy brick apartment houses, no grass, some asphalt basketball courts with netless rims slipped forward from slam dunking. Knots of teenage boys sat tensely on porch steps or stood on street corners, getting high on pot, staring at passing cars like they were deciding which ones to grenade.

I pulled into a Clark station. Filled the Skylark with gas. For some promotion, the station had orange leather pylons the shape of pie slices running on ropes from the top of the office to the top of the pumps. As I squeezed the trigger of the nozzle, I listened to the pieces of leather above me make hard slaps like laundry.

I told Elvia to use the bathroom even if she didn't have to. Then I did. I have a two-quart, wide-mouth mason jar between the front and back seat to use on stakeouts when the bladder can't take the pressure any longer, but obviously we wouldn't use that this time.

I bought a carton of Kools and a DuPrey street map for a buck fifty. In the car, I spread the map across the steering wheel like a tablecloth. I located Wilson Street, which was the street I wanted. We were roughly a mile north of it.

Five minutes later, we turned on it off Jensen Boulevard. It was immediately apparent that even DuPrey had an area so down and out that the rest of town could call it the armpit of the city, and Wilson was it.

It was only four blocks long and curved slightly to the right along its length and then dead-ended in front of a three-story brick building. The houses were all wood and as small as garages. Most looked like the next windstorm would be their last.

I drove the four blocks just checking things out, not looking at addresses or anything. The brick building was a school. Espinosa Elementary. An upside down Satan's fork was spray painted in orange on the fan-shaped front door and Spanish words were in red above it. There was other graffiti in other colors running at schoolboy height all across the front of the school. I pointed at the door and asked Elvia what the words meant.

She read it, then said slowly, "The Latin Deuce Killers own you."

"Ooh, we're going to have a real fun time hanging out here. What about the other words?"

She shrugged. "Gang names mostly."

I turned around in the playground at the side of the school and drove back down Wilson. Middle of the third block, right side, was 333, the number on the paper Medina had given me. The house was the biggest on the street, a two-story Victorian in a saggy shambles with plywood boards covering the upstairs windows, a patch of dirt serving for a front lawn. The sign and words from the school door were painted the length of the porch.

Across the street from 333 and down four houses was a small

Spanish food store. *Cerveza fria* signs hung behind three windows and behind burglar bars that stretched across the front door. The burglar bars were unlocked and slightly open, so I decided the store was open for business. All the other signs on the store, including the one proclaiming the store's name, were hand painted in red and green letters on white wood by someone who was not a professional sign painter. Squiggly slivers of red and green paint slid from each letter on each sign like thread on a suit that needed to be nipped.

I said, "We'll park in front of the store, facing the other way. You may have to go in the store once in a while. We'll drive around the neighborhood some, we may even have to neck some." I looked at Elvia and we both laughed. "We have to act like we got a reason to be here. I didn't think it would be so deserted." I turned around in a driveway and parked in front of the store.

I reached under the seat for the brandy bottle. Still a little left. I took a sip. A stakeout is a hard thing when you've got speed sparking the nervous system. You want to *move*, Jack. I was glad I'd kept it to three. But there was a reason I ate them. Speed makes me feel the hell-with-it brave when I mix it with alcohol. Not being a supremely courageous man by nature, I take my backbone where I find it.

I drumrolled my fingers on the steering wheel, punched radio buttons one-two-three like Stacey Ford. After only twenty minutes, Elvia needed a break. She went to the store. I shouted after her to pick up a newspaper. She came back with five Snickers bars, two Diet Pepsi's and four Chicago Spanish newspapers that were two days old. She laughed, said, "This is it. Want me to read to you?"

I had *La Voz de Chicago* in my hand. I said, "I'll pretend." Elvia told me it meant the Voice of Chicago, which I could've figured on my own. I propped it on the steering wheel, gave it my utmost concentration.

At 11:30, a squad car pulled behind us. I'd been waiting for it. I laid the newspaper over the paraphernalia on the seat, stuck the brandy bottle under it. A black cop with a face so young looking he resembled a junior high kid dressed up as a policeman came to my window. He said he had a call about us and wanted to know what was up.

I said, "Just waiting for some friends." I nodded at Elvia. "My wife and I are wanting to rent that house." I pointed at one across the street from the store. "Our friends own it, plan to show us through. They're late, but they'll show."

He turned to look at the house, then gave a long look up and down the street, then his eyes settled on my face. He said, "If I might offer some free advice, sir, you and your wife don't want to even consider living on Wilson Street. Anywhere this side of town, to tell the truth."

"You haven't been a cop long, right?"

"Six weeks. How'd you know?"

"The 'sir.' Rookies talk like that for a very short time."

He looked embarrassed, smiled a little.

I said, "We're from Chicago. Uptown. We want to escape the crime and gangs in there. It's real brutal. We're wanting to start a family, but it's not healthy to do it where we live."

The cop's face broke out in a wide grin. "To escape the crime in Chicago, you move to DuPrey? Wilson Street no less." He slapped the windowsill, started laughing like Eddie Murphy. He walked slowly back to the squadrol. He was still laughing as he pulled around us.

Shortly after noon, Cesar Lopez was suddenly there. Walking in the street next to my car. I'd let my mind wander and hadn't seen him leave the house so when he and another Hispanic man walked past my door, I jumped off the seat like the sharp tip of a spring had poked through it. The men went into the grocery store.

I muttered, "Damn, I wanted him to be alone."

Elvia said, "Should we wait until he is?"

"I'm sick of waiting. This might be our only shot."

I decided on the mace. I was sticked once and I don't care to inflict that kind of pain on anyone unless they're inflicting pain on me. I put it in my left hand just in case. I lifted up and stuffed a pair of cuffs in my back pocket, one ring in, one ring dangling. Grabbed the mace can with my right hand.

Three minutes later, both men left the store. Each carried a twelve-pack of Corona. They came right at us.

When they were even with the front of the Skylark, I opened my door. I had each hand cupped under so the baton and mace can were concealed behind each arm. The men looked at me, but I held my eyes on the store like that was my destination.

I maced his friend first. A long stream directly in his face. I was lucky the wind was at my back so none of it blew back on me. The man collapsed to the street like he'd just seen God, clawing his eyes, gasping air.

Lopez froze for a second, stared down at his friend. He dropped the twelve-pack, started to run to my left across the street. I moved quickly even with him, spun him around by the arm with the stick. Gave him a squirt that dropped him to his knees. He struggled up and started to move slowly forward, unable to see. I tossed the can and stick through my window into the car, grabbed Lopez by the arm and ran him to the Skylark. Shoved him forward against the back door. I shouted, "Police, smack the top of the car." Just like I used to.

He slapped his hands on the car roof. I kicked his left ankle sideways. Said, "Spread the feet. More." I kicked his ankle until he was in a position where if he tried to move, all he could do was fall backwards.

I had the cuffs in my right hand. I grabbed his left hand, bent it behind him, cuffed it. I lifted that hand up his spine until he yelled. I wrenched his right hand behind him, brought his left hand down until they almost touched and slipped the right cuff on. Took only seconds. I work fast when I'm scared.

I pulled Lopez away from the car, opened the back door, pushed him roughly inside. He fell face down on the seat. I yelled, "Crawl up, get your feet in."

His friend was standing now, but couldn't see where he was going. He moved away from us, still in the street, clawing air.

I walked over and picked up Lopez' twelve-pack, threw it on his back, slammed the door.

Behind us men were shouting Spanish. A gun fired, then another. I had the Skylark moving in seconds, gunning it down Wilson, swerving hard to avoid Lopez's buddy who still struggled forward, arms outstretched like a zombie emerging from a graveyard.

There were more shots and suddenly I couldn't see out the

rear window. It was glazed over with thousands of silvery lines.

I took a left at the dead end in front of the school. Turned a different way at the next four corners. Saw no pursuing cars so I slowed to thirty. I did not need to be pulled over at this time for speeding. The rear window was going to be invitation enough.

After I slowed, Elvia sensed we were safe for now. She turned and shouted at Lopez. He answered in Spanish, machine gunning words at her. He sounded scared as hell. I shouted, "Shut up!" over the seat and he did.

I said, "I know you asked him about the money. What's he saying? He speak English?"

She talked to him. He answered. She said, "He says very little. Before, he was saying he doesn't know anything about a bag of money or my brother or a hotel in Chicago. He wants to know if you're really the police."

"Quit talking to him."

"But, Dan, if he has the money."

"You wanna go back to that house and get it?"

She turned and faced forward, said, *"Damn!"*

There was silence the rest of the way to Chicago except for the popping sounds I made when opening a new can of Lopez's beer, and the sneezes and gags Lopez made because of the mace.

Two hours after I'd thrown Cesar Lopez into the back seat, I double parked in front of the Elizabeth Hotel. I told Elvia that if the desk clerk was an old man wearing a Cubs cap, she was to give him ten bucks and ask him to join me for a brief chat.

A minute later, they walked down the three cement steps and across the sidewalk. The man had on the cap, a gray sweatshirt, clown-baggy brown slacks and black rubber galoshes unbuckled. The kind your mom made you wear to school when it was cloudy.

He came to the window, recognized me, made a face. Elvia got back in the car. I told her to tell Lopez to look at us. She did. He groaned and maneuvered and eventually sat up. Tears still ran down his face and he was blinking hard.

I asked the hotel man, "Ever see this man before?"

The man looked at Lopez, then at me, then dropped his gaze. I said, "Elvia, give the man another ten."

She leaned across me and he plucked the sawbuck from her hand. He said, "Sure. I remember the mark on his face."

I said, "This is the scarred guy who came in shortly before the gangbangers did to see Ricardo Reyes, right? You told me you rented 216 to a faggot looking for a room to get his rocks off in. But what really happened was he asked for Ricardo's room number same as the rest of us, then hightailed it upstairs."

"He gave me ten bucks not to talk so I didn't."

"You knew this guy killed Reyes and didn't tell the police or me because of ten bucks?"

"Fuck all you guys. I gave my word."

"So why talk now?"

"Twenty bucks is more than ten bucks and I can still lie to the police. Remember what I said about if you go to the law?"

"That hallway that runs to the right of your cage? Leads to a side or a back exit, right?"

"This guy left that way after he came back down the stairs, didn't he?"

"Might have."

I said, "That's all I need to know." The man turned and walked back to his hotel. He had the door open, about to enter when I yelled, "One more thing. You speak Spanish?"

Over his should he said, "Hell, no."

I turned and looked at Lopez. Said, "That means you speak English."

He was shivering hard, hands locked at his back, watery eyes staring down. He said, "So fucking what."

And your name *is* Cesar, if I remember correctly, but it isn't Cesar Lopez."

He didn't answer, kept staring at the floor of the car.

There was a pay phone at the curb in front of the hotel. I called Medina's number. This time he was waiting by the phone for me. I told him I'd be at the garage in an hour.

FORTY-THREE

Medina stood in front of the garage doors, arms folded, wearing faded jeans and a gray long sleeve sweat shirt. The wannabe Kings weren't playing sentinel across the street.

I pulled Cesar out of the back seat and stood him up. He kept his head down like a Mafia boss evading cameras. With my hand tight around his elbow, I directed him around the car toward the doors. He looked up then and saw Medina. He made a frightened noise, tried to wrestle away, but I kept my right hand tight on his elbow and cuffed him alongside the head with my left and he got quiet.

Medina led us through the garage. The panel vans were still parked on the far side and the sour sweat smell still floated in the gassy air. No naked teenage girls. I was disappointed.

Two men waited for us in the office. They sat on folding chairs on each side of the desk, facing each other, their feet underneath the bottom of the desk. I was expecting them both: Luis Santiago and Nick Toreldo. I didn't know what was going to happen or where I stood; Toreldo might've convinced Medina and Santiago I had to go. But I had no choice but to take the chance. I was low on options. I tried not to show how much seeing Toreldo scared me. I unlocked the cuffs, set them on the desk. Said, "Luis, I brought your brother back."

Luis stared at Cesar, Elvia and me as we stood in front of Medina just inside the door. He smiled his TV smile. He had on his uniform, a pin-striped gray suit, white shirt, burgundy tie. Hair was perfect. He looked like he was waiting for a director to say "Ten seconds, Mr. Santiago." He said, "Thanks, Dan. You do good work. But we've all known that for a while now."

Toreldo wore a trench coat. He was laying the evil eye on me. His voice steady he said, "What the fuck's this I hear you debated putting out a contract on me? You thought about fingering ME?" His voice rose with his rage and he half stood, upper torso bent forward, index and middle finger pointing. "You wanted to cash my ticket, you two-bit punk?"

I said, "Nothing personal, Nicky."

Luis Santiago said quietly, "Shut up, Nick." Toreldo shut up. Santiago said, "Elvia, come here."

Toreldo sat down, staring hatred at me. Elvia walked around me to Santiago, stood next to him. He motioned her to bend forward. She put her ear next to his mouth. He whispered something. She shook her head. My stomach sank like a rock in a river. The odds of my walking out of this room were roughly the same as a cat barking. Toreldo saw the fear grow in my eyes and chuckled.

Medina locked the door, took Cesar's arm and walked him to, then pushed him into the vinyl bottomed chair, just behind Toreldo. The chair I'd sat in yesterday, agreeing to the scheme that put me in the mess I was in now. Cesar still shivered, goosebumps covered his bare arms. If I could've forgotten the sight of Ricardo Reyes' gaping neck, I might've felt sorry for him.

Looking at me, Luis Santiago said, "Elvia Reyes is my dear friend, Dan. If that saddens you, I'm sorry. She developed a case of temporary insanity last week when she saw the money. She stole what she delivered to Finney for me, although I blame him more than her. Then, still temporarily insane which was caused by greed, she hired you to get it back for her. But soon after that I talked to her and she came to her senses."

I said, "She started a lot of trouble."

"Not really. It was all trouble I wanted to happen sooner or later. So it happened now." He made a big shrug. "It's good to get it over with. And quick like this is better."

I said, "I got the drift of what was happening the last few days. I even figured you into it because the Kings showed up when there was no good reason for them to except that I had talked to you and said I wanted to see them. And you asked so many questions when I talked to you. You wanted to know exactly what I knew about everything. And then last night, I remembered you telling me about your brother that night we got drunk on Blue Island. How he had this mark on his face and you felt sorry for him because he was self-conscious about it and people made comments. But I didn't suspect Elvia."

Elvia wouldn't look at me. She stood like a statue next to Luis Santiago and stared at the middle of the desk.

Luis said, "When she called me yesterday while you were here with Enrique, she told me what's been going on between you two. I'm sure you didn't want to suspect Elvia. She delivered a suitcase of money from me to Finney. Some of it was his payoff, some of it was for other people. Orlando left it unattended and didn't put it in his safe like he should of. That's why I blame him. Never put temptation in front of the poor. But all he wanted was to get laid and go to sleep. Elvia came upon the suitcase and, temporary insanity. She stuffed the money in a grocery bag and split. But I forgive her. All my friends get one strike with me. Besides, she volunteered to keep an eye on you to make things right. I didn't like the idea of you stumbling around in this, but so long as I knew what you were up to, it was okay. She kept me informed, so I forgave her." He put his arm around her waist, hugged tight. She blinked but didn't move or speak.

I said, "I know a lot of what's happening here. I know you're involved in the drug trade on the West Side and you, of course, desperately need front men. Cantel and Finney were your front men for awhile. But I learned you recently acquired a connection in Miami who'll supply you with all the heroin and cocaine you can get rid of. That makes the wetback taxi pipeline obsolete. I know you planned to shove Cantel and Finney out the door. I think you brought your brother back from Mexico City to run things. Low key of course. Medina and the Kings are your strong men. Not a bad set up. Too bad your brother had to fuck up big-time."

Luis moved his eyes to Cesar. Said, "My brother indeed fucked up big-time. But that means opportunity strikes for Enrique, eh Ricky? You know, I understand a farm girl going off the deep end the first time she sees a lot of money, but not a businessman. Elvia had carried the suitcase back and forth before, but she'd never actually seen what was inside until that one time. But a businessman who can't ignore huge amounts of cash is essentially—useless."

I said, "Cesar, why'd you run to a dump in DuPrey when you got God knows how much money in your hands? You could of gone anywhere."

Still staring at his brother, Luis said, "It was twenty grand in the bag, Dan. Twenty big. But after this happened, I called some friends in Mexico City and I learned a lot about my little brother. I wish I had known these things before I brought his worthless carcass north. I paid big money—money I didn't always have—to send him to University down there so he could get an education. He studied business, English, math, communications, all the courses a good businessman needs to take. I wished I would of had the same opportunity when I was his age. But Cesar also learned to take drugs at University. In fact, that's what he learned best of all. He hung out with the gangs who supplied the drugs. Many of these gang people have since crossed and some now live in DuPrey. On Wilson Avenue. I learned about the cocaine he is addicted to. He ran to DuPrey so he and his amigos from Mexico City could smoke and snort cocaine for as long as twenty big would last."

Cesar's head was bent forward almost to his knees. He sobbed quietly. Like me, he knew there were some long odds happening in the room. And they were getting longer. Toreldo quit staring at me, turned around to give Cesar a quick look. Turning back, he made a noise low in his throat. Said, "Quit bawlin', sissy. You fuck up, you gotta pay for it. That's the rules."

I said, "So Cesar went with some Romeo Kings to the Elizabeth Hotel to get the money back. He went in alone and killed Ricardo when he saw the cash. That money was cocaine to him. Green was white. That makes 'drug sense.' He didn't come out the front after five minutes so the Kings outside knew something was not good. One of them went inside and found Reyes. How'd you know Reyes was there?"

Luis said, "Finney told me. Finney hadn't figured out yet his time had come and gone. He had no vision. He was content to keep everything small-time because that's exactly what he was. Small-time. He was more interested in wetbacks than heroin. He was content with an unimaginative thug like Cantel for his partner." He shook his head. "Thinking he was still inside, Finney called me as soon as he realized Elvia took the money. Elvia told me her brother had taken it from her and Ford told Finney where Ricardo stayed. Like he told you."

I said, "Too bad for Ford that when I rattled that same information out of him, he suspected something big was up and he got those delusions of grandeur. You ever feel bad about all this, Luis? A lot of people would feel betrayed if word of this ever got around."

"Sure, sometimes I feel bad. Sometimes I lay awake at night and it haunts me. But in the morning I'm okay. Because you got to realize the ends justify the means. Lots of the money goes back into the community, and some year soon, I'll go back to Mexico and spend so much on my people, it'll be worth it."

"Keep telling yourself that. Maybe one day you'll believe it. You're gonna turn out just like the people you told me about. You won't know when to say enough is enough. You'll never go back. How'd you start this?"

"Gradually. At first, Finney and smaller dealers like Enrique gave me small payoffs here and there so I wouldn't louse the action by getting the community overly riled about drugs. Token amounts to not be a hardliner. It was no big deal because I'm realistic enough to know that poor people are gonna get high whether I say no or not. And the money helped. I didn't have much, what with sending Cesar to school and all. You don't make much money when you have to depend on donations from people living in one of the poorest sections of Chicago. Eventually I realized how much money was getting made. And then I observed how stupid most of these people were. I cultivated the biggest street gang in Pilsen for my foot soldiers and I started to make deals and contacts out of state. I eased myself into the operation. The last six months I've gotten more involved. Finney and some others didn't approve so I decided they were history. Elvia set it all in motion a little early and, yes, Cesar proved himself to be totally worthless, but it's still going to work out. We can make money for ourselves *and* our community."

I said, "That part of the community that isn't strung out or killed anyway. So I just happened to get hired into the case right when this power struggle broke out. Kruger luck strikes again. Once Ford did get thinking, he figured things out quicker than Finney. I don't think Finney knew he was done for until that chase down Lincoln. After that, he was desperate for that money so he could get the hell out of here. Ford went to the Elizabeth after I forced the location out of him, found out the Kings had been there, too. So Finney had asked him, I'd asked him, and the Kings were involved. He knew something was up. He started playing three ends against the middle, figuring to cover his ass no matter who came out on top. I suspect it was his idea to get me and Cantel together."

Luis said, "No, it was mine. I knew you'd find out about the heroin coming out of the back office at the Midnight Lounge. I thought sure you'd turn Cantel in to the police. I tried to push you along in that direction. That would save us from killing him. He was so small-time all he knew about was Finney and a few flunkie Kings who picked up and delivered. And Finney was going to die, so Cantel could talk his ass off to the law for all I cared. But I found out you're not the type of cop who automatically turns drug dealers in."

Toreldo said, "But there's one thing about Cantel. He is *real* scared of prison. He did a stretch in Joliet years ago and he did not want to ever go back. The inmates sexual practices did not turn him on. He couldn't figure out what was happening with Ford having him hire you to flush Finney when Ford was hanging out with Finney at the time. He immediately got thoughts like set-up, bust, and prison. So he freaked, killed four dealers he got hooked up with 'cause of Ford, then split town. He was so scared, he hired some two-bit PI to check on things when he couldn't get a hold of me right away. I wish he'd of waited and found me."

Luis said, "We didn't know about you, Nick. We didn't know Cantel wasn't as small-time as we thought."

"It's okay, I ain't sore. I go with the odds. Cantel was decent enough, but dumb as they come. So dumb he thought he was smart. This'll work out better. We got brains now. We got the front, the protection, soldiers, the works."

I said, "Why'd you kill Ford?"

"I popped Ford and the junkie nigger bitch you stashed at Alice Baker's apartment because they knew Cantel had killed the four South Siders."

"Why'd you go to Baker's apartment?"

"Cantel called his PI and the PI told him he'd talked to somebody when he called the apartment. Somebody pretending to be Cantel. Course the ignorant PI thought it *was* Cantel. Cantel asked me to check it out. The junkie bitch told me you'd seen Cantel go into some apartment and kill one of the the pushermen, so I was looking for you. You can imagine how Cantel reacted when he heard that. You must of thought you were one smart SOB having her crash at Alice's place." He winked. "Wasn't half bad actually. She could of stayed there forever if you hadn't picked up the phone."

I said. "I didn't know about you either, Nick. And I don't understand why you were so loyal to a two-bit pusher like Joseph Cantel. You being a narcotics cop and all."

The sarcasm was lost on Toreldo. He bristled, made a noise of contempt. "Loyal to Cantel? Wanna see how loyal I am?"

He reached down on his right, lifted up, then smacked a pebbled black briefcase onto the desk, slid open the two locks. He said, "This is Cantel's runaway money. Twenty-five grand left. Luis, I want to demonstrate my good faith. I hope this new partnership is long and prosperous for all of us. This is a gift to you from me."

I said, "Typical dago grandstand play. Toreldo, you are an A-one ass kisser. How'd you get Cantel's money?"

Toreldo removed a small manila envelope from his trench coat pocket. Slid it across the desk to Luis who opened it and remove some photographs. Luis looked at them for some seconds, nodded and slid them toward me.

There were three color Polaroids of Joseph Cantel and Alice Baker. They were lying naked side by side on their backs on a wooden floor. Each had three bullet holes in their chest. Lines of blood leaked from the holes to the floor, mingling into a puddle between them. Toreldo hadn't shot the heads because he wanted us to make the ID. In the bottom photo, the hands of Cantel and Baker were missing. Their arms ended at the wrists in bloody stumps. The hands had been placed above the heads and all four bent inward, clawlike. I understood the reason for this photo. You can fake a photo of death by gunshot, but you can't fake an amputation.

Luis said, "Thank you, Nicholas. For the gift and for the removal of Joseph Cantel. After Enrique talked to Dan yesterday and then got in touch with you, I wasn't sure how'd you react. But everything is smooth now."

Toreldo said, "Like I said, I go with the odds. Must be the dago in me, eh Kruger? I know two people ain't walkin' outta this office. Let Kruger be mine, okay Luis?" He kept his eyes on me, grinning wide.

Which was a mistake. While staring at me, Toreldo paid no attention to Luis as Luis started talking again. Luis said, "However, while you *have* been a help to us, Nick, I have to believe that if you turned on Joseph Cantel, you'd turn on us sooner or later if the odds shifted. Besides, I'd prefer not to have any of Cantel's people around anymore." He looked at me, said, "You want to argue about this with me, Dan?"

Towards the end of Luis' talk, the words began to penetrate Toreldo's brain. His grin vanished and his eyes swerved from me to Luis Santiago. He jammed his left hand inside his trenchcoat and started to push away and stand.

Then the top of his head exploded in red and white and gray as Medina fired a revolver from six inches away, on Toreldo's blind side. Blood and brains splattered against one of the Spanish dance posters on the wall.

Cesar and Elvia each made a quick involuntary scream. I went numb. Toreldo fell sideways. There wasn't enough room between the chair and the wall for him to fall to the floor. He leaned against the wall, half on, half off the chair, the part of his head that was left tilted awkwardly back on his shoulder.

Cesar stood up from his chair, eyes berserk with fear. Luis said, "*Adios, hermano.*"

Enrique shot Cesar twice in the chest. Cesar slammed against the wall. He started to brush his lapel like a bullet in the chest was something he could flick off his shirt to the floor. He stared at Luis, not realizing he was dead. Then he fell forward. His face banged off the backrest of the chair Toreldo was in and he came to rest sitting on the floor, the back of his head leaning against the front of the chair he'd sat in.

Enrique pivoted toward me. I was next. But then Luis screamed. He screamed again as Elvia brought a brick down on his head. He tried to stand, but couldn't because his legs were trapped under the edge of the desk. He made it inches off the chair, but no further. Blood slid down the sides of his head and face like someone had cracked a red egg on his skull. Again

Elvia slammed the brick down with both hands and the light faded from Luis' eyes. He slumped back in the chair, head lolling.

Medina had frozen, as mesmerized as I was watching Luis die. I bent and lunged at his waist like a linebacker sacking a QB. The room was so small, I had him against the wall right away. I grabbed the wrist of his gun hand and pushed straight up, used my weight to hold him against the wall. The gun went off, as deafening as summer thunder. I grabbed his belt, with my right hand, pushed forward. Medina fell onto Cesar's body and the vinyl bottom chair. The chair toppled over. I fell on top of Medina.

He yelled Spanish words and tried to flex his body to flip me off. Outweighing me by one hundred pounds, it would've been easy except he was cramped for space and was using a dead man and a fallen chair as a base to work from. It must have been like trying to high jump off a sack of potatoes.

I used my body and left arm to keep Medina pinned. I reached up with my right hand, felt around the shelf above us for one of the trophies. My hand found one and I rammed the base of it against his head three times. He grunted the first two times, after the third time he stopped moving. I felt his carotid artery. He wasn't dead, only out cold.

I started to breathe again, fast and ragged. My heart was doing four-four in my throat. I untangled myself from the two bodies and the chair. Pushed to my feet.

I looked at Elvia. She was pointing a gun at me.

I said, "Luis' gun?"

She nodded. She looked scared and confused, but I knew better than to assume she was too scared to shoot. I said, "You don't want to kill me."

"No, I don't. Is Enrique dead?"

"No."

"Tie him up."

"Why?"

Her voice got loud. "Tie him up, I said. His arms. Very tight. Put a rag in his mouth."

There was rope on a table in the garage. I stepped outside the door to get it, then wrapped it around Medina's chest and arms and made two knots. I put the chair upright, lifted Medina into it and ran more rope around his torso and the chair a lot of times. Tied two more knots. I opened his mouth, situated a doubled-in-half clean blue rag in it. It was a large rag and I pulled it behind his neck and tied it. I put my ear next to his nose for a bit. He was breathing okay.

I looked at Elvia again. The gun still pointed at my chest. Cantel's briefcase of money was on the floor by her feet. She said, "I'm sorry, Dan."

"We aren't partners anymore?"

"Not anymore. Put your hands behind you."

There was a light clinking of metal and the cuffs were around my wrists and locked. She removed the key from my jacket pocket. She took a length of leftover rope, wrapped it around the link between the cuffs, then took it to the desk and ran it many times around the desk leg on the other side and tied it.

While she did, I said, "Elvia, don't let me rot in here. These dead men may be the only people who come here on a regular basis. Especially now that the taxi service is finished. Take off for Tocambaro. Live like a queen, dump on everybody who dumped on you, but call somebody to get me out of here. Even if you wait a day or two. I won't turn you in."

She didn't say anything. She turned on another lamp that stood on the shelf and made a slow turn in the tiny room, looking for something she might've missed. Then she bent down and kissed me softly on the lips. She removed my car keys from my pants pocket. She whispered in my ear, "I really am sorry, Dan, but it's business, okay? Your car'll be at the first auto dealer I come to. I saw some plates on the table when we came in. I'll have them put on my new car. Goodbye."

She left.

Immediately time dragged. I thought of the Muddy Water song with the line, 'The minutes seem like hours, the hours seem like days.'

I wondered what Elvia would do. There was no reason for her to call anybody to get me out. I knew where she was headed. I'd told her I wouldn't talk, but why should she take the chance? Maybe she couldn't bring herself to kill me in cold blood, but this way she could tell herself she'd given me a chance. And if fate decided I should starve to death in a blood-filled garage in Little Village, so be it. Que sera, sera. As time trudged by like a depression, my feelings teeter-tottered. For while I was convinced I was a dead man. Then I'd tell myself *somebody* had to visit this garage in the next two weeks.

Sometime, many hours later, Medina came to. His eyes were screaming. He didn't move or make any sounds. He looked at me. There was some anger and confusion in his eyes, but mostly pain. I could think of nothing to say to him so I looked away. About an hour later, he went under again.

I nodded off for awhile, woke up freezing. My arms were dead as firewood and that scared me. I would've given five years for a Valium and a Kool. Four years for just a Kool.

Later, when I had calculated it'd been twenty-four hours since Elvia left, four uniform cops charged through the office door. Three went to check on the dead men and Medina. One undid the cuffs and told me a woman had phoned in an anonymous tip about the garage. I asked the time. It was only twelve hours since Elvia had left, but that meant she was more than halfway to Tocambaro.

I started to wonder what I was going to tell the police. I wanted Elvia to make it.